Emosional Atyachar

Emosional Atyachar

Every man dies, not every man really lives

Ankit Uttam

General Press

Published by
GENERAL PRESS
4228/1, Ansari Road, Daryaganj
New Delhi – 110002
Ph. : 011 – 23282971, 9911359970
e-mail : generalpressindia@gmail.com

First Edition : November 2011

ISBN : 9789380914121

Edited by Manju Gupta
Cover designed by Sanjay Verma

To purchase our books online, please log on:
www.flipkart.com
www.infibeam.com

Published by Azeem Ahmad Khan for General Press
Printed by Jaico Printers, New Delhi

Dedication

To all my crushes, flings and heartbreaks.
Kal, aaj aur kal.

Acknowledgement

This final product, which you are holding in your hand, is a result of the hard work of many persons and this holds true even today, not only for this book but for any other book too.

To start with, for my second Academy Awards speech, I would again like to express my appreciation to all my mentors who knowingly or unknowingly mentored me by their actions and words.

I would not have been what I am today without the support of the written and spoken words of wisdom by Ayn Rand, Earl Nightingale, Robert Kiyosaki, Stephen King, Dean Koontz, Lee Child and Tom Clancy.

{Round of applause}

The list continues with gratitude to my parents, my brother Kalpit and Motya.

{Round of applause continues.....}

The next set of names includes those who not only helped me but also encouraged me while writing this book – Archana Pandey ma'am (sorry for forgetting to include this name last time), Dhawan, my partner Aditi, Shuchi, Sneha ma'am, Sapna *Didi*, my on-and-off friend Shubhangi, my team-mates Amita, Aarti and Manoj.

Ladies and gentlemen, without your support, this book would never have taken shape.

{More round of applause}

I would like to thank General Press for giving me this opportunity to show my disabilities once again to the world and especially Mr Azeem for being a very supportive publisher, an even better friend and a splendid human being.

I can't finish this note without thanking God for gifting me with this life which has never ceased to amaze me and for allowing me to follow my heart in times of adversity.

There are numerous other names which I, due to my forgetful nature, might have missed, but that should not prevent you from reminding me by sending me an e-mail at ankit.uttam@gmail.com. You can also send your comments, thoughts or any questions that you may have in mind to the same id.

Hope you will enjoy reading this book as much as I enjoyed writing it.

Preface

Everything has been figured out, except how to live.

—Jean-Paul Sartre

Prologue

The clock struck eleven with a soft sound.

Vimarsh lay on the bed, while Nick sat beside him, reading a newspaper.

"Who brought me here?" Vimarsh asked delicately, expecting a sarcastic reply.

"You swallowed 43 pills in one shot…fuckin extraordinaire," but didn't get one.

"Why did you save me?" he continued with his slim odds.

"If you really want to know…okay…I don't want any fuckin legal headaches because of your failed suicide attempts in our flat. And you owe me five thousand fuckin bucks for keeping your idiocy out of police records," Nick smiled. "Next time, try jumping from some building or bridge for demonstrating your fuckin wisdom."

Vimarsh felt each word, from Nick, biting deep into his skin.

"Hello Mr. Vimarsh, I am glad Nick brought you here on time. How are you feeling now?" the doctor asked, entering into the room.

Vimarsh felt a sudden urge to strangle Nick till his eyeballs bulged out from their beloved adobes.

"Thanks Shiva for providing help at the right juncture and keeping this case out of bounds for the police," Nick acknowledged, looking genuinely grateful. Vimarsh was surprised at the sudden discovery of some new emotions in Nick's wallet of emoticons.

"Shiva and I are college friends. I never knew he was working in this hospital until yesterday when I saw his fuckin name on the doctors' list."

"You have not changed even a bit," Shiva smiled.

"Excuse me, doctor," a nurse interrupted their small talk.

༁ᢀ༉

"Vimarsh, who else is there in your family?"

"No one. My parents died in a car accident six years ago and after that, I haven't had any connection with any of my relatives."

"So your family only consists of Nick?"

Vimarsh said nothing.

"What happened? Is there anything wrong?" Nick asked.

"Nick, I don't know how to say it?"

"What's happened, doctor?" Vimarsh asked, looking real worried.

"Actually Vimarsh, your blood test report has something, I mean… something…which was not expected."

"Doctor, can you stop posing these riddles and tell me what the matter is exactly?"

"Vimarsh, there is a kind of blood contamination. Normally this happens due to prolonged radiation, but in your case we still are not sure how you got affected."

"Is it serious? I mean it is curable…right?"

"There is no need to worry. We are also seeking a second opinion from the specialists in Mumbai. Did you ever face any temporary blackouts accompanied with excruciating headaches or stomach-aches?"

"Yeah, sometimes it has happened but lately the frequency has increased. I think it is because I work on my laptop continuously for long hours. But this could not be the reason…right?"

"Vimarsh, when the battery in the laptop gets considerably old, it starts emitting certain kinds of radiation, but we are not sure if that is the reason. There are various other plausible reasons."

"But it is curable, right?"

"Yes, it is curable if detected early. In the worst case, even blood transfusion doesn't work. One can only hope to live to a maximum of four to five months."

"You mean I only have four months?"

"I didn't mean that. I was only telling you about the worst case scenario," Shiva said, suddenly on the back foot.

"Life has never been fair to me. Now I have only four months to live. I always knew that I am going to die," Vimarsh said, now beginning to cry.

"Stop crying like a fuckin baby. Nothing is gon'na happen to you," Nick finally opened his mouth, but looked absolutely shell shocked at the sudden turn of events.

1

❧ · ❧

Yesterday, 11:45 p.m.

"One…two…three…four…five…six," I counted and arranged six pills tidily near the table lamp.

"Suicide – that's the only option left in my life – a life which sucks. I know suicide is an offence punishable under Section 309 of the Indian Penal Code. Of course, I googled it just in case someone were to come forward and save me. I should at least be aware of my sentence. I think there are people out there who would be interested in knowing the reasons behind my decision merely from a gossip point of view rather than sympathising with my agony. So, for their information, the reason for my suicide took birth thirty-three years ago."

Part I

Vishvesh Krishnamurthy Ramanathan

2

Thirty-three years ago

Somewhere in Tamil Nadu

"Mr. Krishnamurthy...congratulations, it's a boy."

A smile stretched on the doting father's face.

"Congrats son...you have done a great job," a face, with freckled cheeks and age written all over it, eulogised over his son's lone achievement in twenty-three years of his life.

"Thanks *amma*," the self-conscious son replied, shyly looking at the surrounding grinning faces.

3

Twenty-five years ago

My birth land

"I was borned in Kattuvelampalayam. It izz a smoll village...no, no...I mean a smoll town in Tamil Nadu. It izz naat like...like it izz naat very smoll but it izz like aukay. I yum feeling so proud to gib a smoll description about my birthland. The Cauvery river runs nearby. Amma told me that it izz very good and we should respect it. She asked me to kaal it Cauvery amma. So I heb one Appa and I heb two Ammas.

It consists of around 500 residencies and one beautiful temple which located at the centre of the village. People are mainly do bizness of veshti and saree and aalso agriculture. Every year, in May, the village peepul celebrates the Amman Festival grandly to say thank you to gawd.

The village made in a very nice way where the roads are constructed well mannered and they behave nicely in rainy season. I know this ass I only go to iskool from that roads only. My school izz very much the most famous in the whole town. I aalways sit next to Maheshwaramma. It izz difficult to gib her describe. But she izz very…like…handsome I can say. She loves me. She aalways gib me her notebook to kaapy fraam my notes. So I know she loves me a laat. I also love her but Amma do naat like her Amma. Her Amma is very bad. I aalso do naat like her Amma.

So many times I aalso get very confuse. From last two days Maheshwar- amma is sitting with her new friend. I do naat like her friend aalso. I am sitting alone. So bad I feeling.

My teacher is very besht. She geeves me home-wok. I finish it in the class wok itself. Then I kaapy it faar Maheshwaramma in her notebook bee-caaz I loves her so many.

I love my town, Amma, Appa and Maheshwaramma."

$\sim \mathbb{G} \mathbb{R}$

Nineteen years passed since that small essay saw the light for the first time on that ruled notebook.

Numerous seasons, several teachers and sometimes students too sat at the very same place where Vishvesh's essay was checked for the first time and his tiny ears were twisted for proclaiming his love for Maheshwaramma in front of the whole class.

Many things had changed in this long gap except for the love interest of Vishvesh Krishnamurthy Ramanathan. He was still franti- cally in love, not with Maheshwaramma, but his muse – the alluring English. He always felt betrayed by Lord Almighty for not having sent him to Mother Earth when India was ruled by the Queen. His belief was that his mastery over the language could be appreciated only by the originals. The left-overs by them were mere numbers for him, now accounting for more than a billion.

The one thing about which he was very peculiar was T.A.T.T.I. which stood for 'Totally Advanced Technical Training Institute' – the institute from where he completed his M.Com. You might wonder how an advanced technical training institute could give a postgraduate degree in commerce; well that is another matter, which is out of the scope of this suicide note.

After passing with flying colours (mostly yellow) from T.A.T.T.I., he joined Anirban Keshto Financial Corporation in Bangalore as a junior accountant. And thus his ascent on the corporate ladder began.

4

Two months ago

The cabin was witnessing yet another episode of pig slaughter.

"NO, NO THIS SHOULD NAAT BE THE CASE."

"Sorry, sir."

"No, no……no sawry……whaat sawry? Aal you peepul (people) have the saeme praablem. Aalways running away from wok (work) and laeter coming to us asking for raiese and promotions," Vishvesh roared at the emaciated-looking clerk.

"But, sir…"

"No……no ifs and no butts. Ass I have told yeveryone in this aaffice that consider wok ass worship and what you peepul are doing…nothing."

"Sorry, sir."

"Sawry never won't mean anything faar me and I do naat geeve no second chances for mishtakes."

Two things Vishvesh absolutely hated — first, when somebody told him that whatever he was saying might not be the correct version. Second, when someone asked him for a holiday — leaves are for work-shirkers, was his belief.

Vishvesh had two main aspirations in his life......

Why are you surprised? Everyone, in my opinion, wants something in his life. Even if you don't agree, it doesn't matter to me since it is my personal suicide note. Write your own if you disagree with mine.

So his first aim was to get the highest salary package ever possible in AKFC and the second was to thwart every attempt to create another managerial post at the Bangalore office. He lovingly called his chair his third love. Well, his second love was to talk down his subordinates in English and to convey to them in no uncertain terms who the real boss was.

He was used to spending two-thirds of his day in the office. But all that changed when in his happening life, something grand happened that too not so long ago......

HE GOT MARRIED!

This could also have been a rumour because no one had ever met or seen his wife alive. I mean she was alive, but I couldn't say it with 100 per cent confidence.

The only proof was the solitary invitation card that was shown to the office as a consolation for not inviting them to the marriage, barring a few, who were invited, but instructed not to divulge this little piece of information to anyone in the office.

Vishvesh had some pretty clear conversation starters for some of the office situations. For his superiors he always used, no matter whatever the request was, "Yeah, yeah, that's a good idea, may be." And for everyone else, his all-time favourite was, "No, no, this should naat be the case." That's how he had been able to maintain his office decorum since the past five years as a manager.

"Ranga, one small *masala* tea. Quick."

"What Samy? Nowadays you seem to be very busy to visit my small shop," said the tea vendor, showing a *paan-masala*-stained toothy grin.

"What to tell, these fucking boss *log* know only one sentence. Samy, bring tea…Samy bring *idli*…Samy bring this…bring that…arghhh."

"Relax Samy."

"Hear this, Sheena ma'am is nowadays teaching loveology to a new intern."

"But last time you told me that she was flirting with some other guy. What was his name?"

"That was yet another sad story. I warned him that she was using him for her advantage but what he did in return? And those who don't pay heed to the advice of ever-ready-to-help Samy, have no future in AKFC. Heart-broken, after she betrayed him, he joined some small company in Pune. I am telling you, one day she will be the manager of this crap company and these truckload of assholes will stand in line, saluting and kissing her hand. In only two years, she has managed to get promoted thrice. She is one helluva sexy bitch. That intern is nowadays working eighteen hours a day, somehow managing to do his task in between her work assignments."

That was Lingasamy. Profession-wise he was a peon but very resourceful within the four walls of AKFC. He specialised in extracting secrets and skeletons in the cupboard of each of his bosses and which were even alien to their best pals and could provide any information provided the price offered met his expectations.

Samy himself had a long list of flings but all his flings finally stopped at Kanyamani, a widow with three children. Their alleged affair ended at Kalyanamantapa, when one night she grabbed his collar and threatened that either he married her or be prepared to be held responsibile for four deaths. Even the most intelligent of men would have done the same which Samy finally settled for.

The skill required in feeding a family of five on a meagre salary of 6,800 rupees in one of the costliest cities of India can only be learned from a peon.

ॐ

"Change *illa*…$*#$#$*#$#@#*#$," followed by some more cuss words in the bus packed with human bodies.

"I don't know Kannada," Vimarsh said, looking helplessly side-ways.

"*Kya paiya, change leke chalne ka naa?* Here also no change."

"Give it to me later. It is still a long way to go till my stop."

The conductor said nothing except to glare at him as if he had asked him for one of his kidneys.

"*Bhaiya*, thirty-five rupees were left," Vimarsh again tried his luck.

"What can I do *paiya?* I have no change."

"Try to get it from somewhere. My stop is about to come."

"From where to get? $*#$#$*#$#@#*#$. Why don't you people keep the change?" the conductor asked, glaring at Vimarsh with his jaundice-affected eyes.

"Okay, I will take it later…some day…maybe," Vimarsh said, while getting off the bus. A wry smile came on the conductor's black face against which his yellow teeth shone.

The bus sped off, leaving behind a splash of wet mud.

That was Vimarsh. Complete name Vimarsh Kant Chaturvedi. Born and brought up in Kanpur *dehat*, Uttar Pradesh. Weight 110 kg. Long, pointed nose. Slightly wheatish in colour with a small unkempt moustache sprouting just beneath his nose. Hair always neatly combed and excess of oil visible on the hair tips. All in all, the worst victim of every fashion faux pas.

Every day at exactly 8:15 a.m., Vimarsh left his flat and after a journey of almost forty-five minutes, he would reach his office.

He was working in AKFC since the past three years, six months and eleven days. Of late, he had been able to enjoy some good moments in his life when he got promoted to the post of accountant. However, the euphoria was short lived just like his little moustache.

Vimarsh stood staring at the speeding bus as all kinds of thoughts, one after another, cropped up and flew across his mind.

It was a MONDAY.

5

"Hello Samy," Vimarsh greeted Lingasamy in a soft tone.

"Late…again!!! Boss is calling you," Lingasamy was busy in crushing *pan masala* on his coarse, freckled palm.

A perfect start to the week.

"Good morning, sir."

Vishvesh glanced at the wall-clock.

"Laete……again!"

"But sir, it's only 8:50; ten minutes early than the regular office timings."

"Hau many times I are told you this…do naat geeve me you-err illaagical reasons."

"But sir…," Vimarsh began, but couldn't continue.

"Do naat interrupt me when I am telling you some things."

"But sir…I always work till late night."

"Mishter, you aar naat the only one who wok haurd here in this aafice. Iph you think so, then you aar very confuse about your value in this aaffice. I think you should take a leaph fraam Sankat who is maadest (modest)…unlike you…but is more haurd-woking than anyone else in this hole aafice. Just remember you aar naat indispensible," Vimarsh felt his heart bleed. "Naau you can go at you-err desk, pleez do naat stand here and waste my time. I just do naat know who promoted you to the post of accountant but nau since you aar one of them, at least try to wok like one. And do naat make me escalaete about your attitude and laete coming habits to the higher manaegement."

"Sorry sir," Vimarsh unwontedly said and left.

5:30 in the evening, and everyone was preparing to leave for the safe confines of their homes.

"Hello…I faargaat to tell you that by tomaarro maarning I want the statements of KrystalKare along with the file," Vishvesh was on the telecom.

"But sir, I had some important work today. I was about to leave now," Vimarsh almost mimicked a goat.

"Listen mishter, do naat give me petty excuses. Whaat heb you done today to aask for such a phavor fraam me? Maarning till evening you just daydream and now you waant me to complete the statements myself? In fact the statements should be at my desk by today only but be-caaz of your wok shirking and laete coming habits it is still pending with you only and now you want to leave early aalso. I do naat waant to know whaat impaartant wok you have but the statements should be at my desk by 9 o'clock, tomaarro," Vishvesh shouted on the phone.

"But sir, you told me that you need it by next Monday."

"So nau you aar telling me that it izz my mishtake?"

"No sir, I didn't mean that."

"Then whaat aar you mean, mishter?"

"Nothing…I will leave after completing it."

"Thank you very, very much," Vishvesh said sarcastically. "I am about to leave nau. Send Sankat in my kaebin."

"But sir, he has already left," said Vimarsh, expecting some form of a downpour on Sankat also.

"Oh, he might be having some impaartant wok. Aukay no praa-blem, I will taalk to him tomaarrow."

Vimarsh toyed with the idea of assassinating Vishvesh with one shot right in between his eyes or may be, between his butts.

෩෧෧

It was 2 o'clock in the night and the office looked more like a morgue. Lingasamy had given the keys to Vimarsh before leaving the office at 6:30. A solitary lamp flickered above his desk.

He was working and then he was working more. His eyes were about to shut tight as if preparing not to open again for any reason or for any of the forthcoming seasons. His head was swivelling like a merry-go-round but at a higher tempo. He was unable to concentrate, so much so that even his fingers pressed the wrong keys on the keyboard. His hands were gradually refusing to move even for a second on the keyboard. With every passing minute he was loathing, more and more, his life and his boss and then again, his life. His back was about to give way. The pain was immeasurable and he felt as if someone was peeling the layers of his skin with a sharp-edged knife, bit by bit. Blood seemed to him to be dripping from his spine and every drop of it was making him realise how much he hated his life and himself for living it.

6

Today 00:10 a.m.

Seven…eight…nine…ten…eleven…five more were added to the already crowded bunch of pills.

But now you might be thinking why I can't leave such a job? But do you really think this is the only reason for this suicide note?

"If you are then, my dear friend, I am afraid you are gravely wrong. Actually this was not at all the reason.

Fortunately the real one was quite attractive, pretty and sexy and did I forget something…yes…a psycho bitch."

Part 2
Sheena

7

~⊛·⊛~

Twenty-two years ago

Father was a high court judge. Stepmother, was a consummate social-ite. Her real mother died when she was barely three-years old. Her father, wrecked due to deprivation of her love, engrossed himself into the heaps of files, leaving his little daughter alone in that large mansion to discover her identity at the tender age.

She was six, when her father, in a bid to make up for the lost time in his daughter's life, got married again and that too to a widow in the hope that already a mother of one, his new soul-mate, would show the same protective attitude towards Sheena as her real mother would have done. So there came a readymade Mom and a brother who was already busy fighting his pubic demons. But she was happy because after a long time someone was going to sing lullabies and fetch her from school.

Now she was no longer lonely in that large closet-like house. Her newfound family was now by her side. But her dream was soon set to shatter when she discovered that her new Mom was more inter-ested in enjoying her new-found status as a magistrate's wife and her new socialite friends rather than preparing the tiffin-box for her new liability. That was the era when the wave of kitty parties had started sweeping the uber rich and the not-so-uber rich off their feet and it was the 'in' thing to get invited to one of those parties. Her brother was already busy fighting with peer group rivalry for attracting the attention of the best girls in school.

Other days she found her Mom dozing off with a cigarette dangling from her fingers, sometimes on the couch, sometimes on the table and at some other times, on the floor. Every party seemed to end like this. Her father knew everything but chose to wear silence. His judgments were lauded in newspapers but his mistakes were visible only on Sheena's face.

In a bid to make up for the mistakes he had committed, he decided to send Sheena to a boarding school, far from the city. It was agonising for him to see his only daughter suffer for his sins.

Sheena, displayed neither the sting of severance nor any sentiments of mercy at her father's incompetence. Her detachment and indifference had long been decided and done. The father-daughter relationship no longer evoked any fervent feelings in her.

School and her aloofness from the social world moulded her into a ruthless and insensate being. She was like a living dead walking among the hoards of crap-loaded minds who still cared about the world at large…*arghhh*.

She found solace in her own company and to fulfil the craving for her highs, she surrounded herself in nicotine-packed environs. She still visited her home but it was only a ritual that she had to comply with every year…twice.

With time she felt changes occur both in her body and also in the eyes of the onlookers. She faced the truth when her stepbrother made a move on her. She should have felt deprecated or ashamed, but as a matter of a shameless fact, she liked it – the attention, the way he looked at her! SHE LIKED IT ALL! Her stepbrother was average looking but the attention of her brother gave her something she had never imagined she would ever get for herself. Their relationship gave them a passport to going out to movies together, restaurants and even sometimes to night clubs where she liked watching the expression on his face when her body slithered against the skin of some stranger.

❦

"I love you, I really do," Chetan was on his knees.

"Isn't it your duty…my sweet brother?" Sheena said while playing with his hair.

It was three in the night and they were in a high-rise nightclub.

"You are gorgeous, I can't live without you."

"Siblings?" Sheena asked tantalisingly.

"I can't stand this relationship any more," Chetan said angrily.

Sheena closed her eyes, experiencing the same kick she got when she took her first drag. Splendid! Enchanting!

The road led nowhere and she didn't intend to reach anywhere. As time passed, in search of new ecstasies, she devised a new diversion, indulging in her unparalleled collection of diverse male libidos while commanding her power over them.

It was not names that mattered to her but the numbers that gave her the satisfaction.

She forbade herself from seeking love any more. It was not to be in her destiny, she had concluded long ago.

Two months ago

"Hi Sheenu…looking so very pretty today."

"Shhh…shhh, don't call me that. I am your supervisor here," Sheena gave Pratyush a mischievous smile.

"As you wish, ma'am. Here are the statement files that you need for today's review meeting."

"Thanks Pratyush, you are such a darling," she softly pinched his cheek.

"Naughty," he said, pleased to receive the unexpected love bite.

"Tonight, let's go out for dinner," she chuckled.

"As you wish…my princess," he shifted his lovey-dovey gaze from her luscious figure which was wrapped in a transparent saree, to the file in his hand.

"Thank you, my *jahanpanaah*," she smiled with a child-like tenderness on her face.

Two years in AKFC and three solid promotions had made Sheena a star in the eyes of the management. Even Vishvesh was in awe of her. She was five feet one inch tall with long black hair and kohl-lined eyes adorning her looks. Her skin was fairly wheatish and she had the knack for exposing her sensuous body through see-through attires worn with stilettos.

Pratyush was the newest jewel in her collection.

So far in her life, she had not missed…not even a single time.

"Where izz that person?" Vishvesh asked.

"He has not yet come," Sankat said with utmost promptness before anyone else.

"It izz 9:15 a.m. and still no sign of his? What he thinks izz this a gorden or aafice? No, no this should naat be the case. Sankat inform me ass soon ass he comes."

"Okay boss," Sankat said, visibly pleased at his victory.

It was 9:45 when Vimarsh reached office, still looking hazy and lost in his previous day's clothes. Apparently he had left the office at 4 in the morning but forgotten to mail anyone about it.

He somehow managed to reach his desk without crashing into anyone else's.

"Samy…water."

"Hi Vimarsh! Boss had summoned you to his room," Sankat said, appearing from nowhere in front of Vimarsh.

Vimarsh looked at him absently.

"Boss has called you in his office," Sankat repeated.

"I heard it," Vimarsh said, looking irritated. "Samy…WATER."

"Go soon," Sankat sternly reminded him before leaving.

Vimarsh looked at him with disgust. His eyes searched for Samy. No sign of him.

"May I come in?"

"Just wait outside….caan't you see that I am in a caanfrence caal with Javier sir."

Javier D'Souja, Vice President of the AKFC was a highly motivated and incurable workaholic. His age had defied all the logics in the history of AKFC. He totally took ten years from the level of a trainee to the post of the V.P. with the much coveted corner office as a symbol of his achievements.

He had recently shifted his base to Bangalore from Mumbai since the two branch offices were not performing well as per his high standards and constantly losing old clients. He mostly worked from the company's old headquarter and took a weekly meeting at the Whitefield office. His main aim was to find some insider who could take up the top post for finance and administration. He had tossed this idea in front of Vishvesh but didn't receive any favourable response from him. He realised the task to get Vishvesh on the same page as he was would have been tough but he had already rejected all the other options for himself.

"Come in," Vishvesh said, still staring at the phone.

"You called me, sir."

"Me? Who told you?"

"Sankat."

"Oh Sankat, yea yea…mishter…," Vishvesh tried to remember the name but failed miserably. "You are agaein laete today. I do naat know what izz it with you? You don't seem to respect anyone's authaarity here. I had told you so MANY times but no paasitive respaanse fraam you-err side."

"Sir, yesterday I went at 4 in the morning," Vimarsh retorted.

"Do naat geeve me excuses. It was you-er mishtake that you did naat complete your wok on time. If this is the case remains then I think I had to taalk to higher shitting pee-pul to demote you."

"But sir…this is unfair," Vimarsh finally opened his mouth after a long hiatus.

"You aar telling that this is unfair but you aar not ready to accept you-er mishtake still?"

"What is my mistake?" he asked, his brain on the verge of exploding.

"Nau you waant me to point out you-er mishtakes aalso? Listen mishter, I am not free like you to waste time on such petty arguments. Whaat you need is inter-inspection, you need to look inside you-er self and find you-er mishtakes. Nau please go and send Sankat inside."

෴

"Yes sir," Sankat was earnest in his greeting.

"Yeah, yeah, Sankat…come in…sit, sit. I waanted to taalk to you about something, too much urgent."

"Sir, I would be lucky if I could be of any help to you."

"Thank you, Sankat. Actually today I spock to Javier sir. He had asked me to find someone who can take the mantle of handling the finance department and that too in six months. Who do you think could be the best caendidate?"

"Sir, I have one very good candidate in my mind," Sankat said, clearing his throat. This was the defining moment.

"Yeah, yeah, tell me Sankat," Vishvesh prodded, beaming with joy. He was, obviously, not expecting such a quick solution to his woes.

"I think Vimarsh will be the best candidate," Sankat said with a poker face.

"Who is Vimarsh? I want someone from our aafice," Vishvesh said, doubting himself over his decision to ask Sankat for a suggestion.

"Sir…Vimarsh……he is our accountant."

"Our accountant…you mean the one whom I just scolded."

"Did he commit any mistake?"

"Mishtake is a very smoll word faar him but I do naat understand whaat are happens to you-er brain?"

Sankat felt offended at the question mark on his grey matter but this was no time to retort.

"Sir, he is the only senior person here whose promotion to the post of the manager is due. Everyone else has already left the company."

"Is that so? Iph that izz the case, then why no one are ever told me this?"

"Sir, you were already very busy, so it might have slipped from your mind."

"Yeah, yeah, you are very correct. I are very buzy nau-a-days."

"Sir, if you think that Vimarsh would not be able to handle this responsibility, then I think you can consider Sheena."

"Sheena!" Vishvesh gave an expression as if he had swallowed a dead mouse. "No, no, I do naat think a woman can handle so much respaansibility. And we need someone who can control peepul."

Sankat gave an excellent performance.

"Sankat, you think about it. If you are need, then go home after lunch, think about this and geeve me some solution after two-three days."

"I will definitely do my best, sir." And the curtain fell.

9

"You are adorable; I am in love with you," Pratyush sat, sitting on the floor at her feet.

Sheena giggled charmingly.

"You never take me seriously," he complained.

"You are too adorable and cute. I just don't feel like saying it. Isn't it so very clear that I like you?"

"Of course it is…my princess."

"I don't want to be a princess. I am no more a princess."

"Then what do you want me to call you?"

"Use your dirty mind," she smiled mischievously.

"A cutie, cuddly baby girl," he tried to gauge yet another of her moods. "I love you baby."

She was sporadically looking unsatisfied with the responses. Her mascara and foundation-coated face was now beginning to reveal her boredom.

Pratyush remembered the last time when he was thrown out of her apartment on failing to appease her demands. He glanced at her nude pink lips and a long-controlled desire to kiss them numbed his mind for a few seconds. His mind dozed off for a while.

"It is not possible," she said irritatingly.

"What's not possible?"

"Whatever you are thinking."

'Did she read my mind?' he wondered.

"Answer my question first," she demanded.

His mind raced hard to think of something that might soothe her. She shifted herself on Pratyush's lap. He moaned instinctively. She rubbed her rear against his pelvis. He found himself shamelessly aroused and widened his legs to make room for her. She casually shifted into the gap. It was hard to concentrate with so much going on.

"Don't you want me?" she asked seductively.

"Very much," he closed her eyes and found himself drifting in the world of lust. He tried to grip her. She rested her back against his body and her hands on his thighs. He looked at her beautiful face with yearning. She was so near, yet he couldn't dare to kiss her.

Her saree slipped from her shoulder, revealing not only her shoulder, but a large part of her neck. She was wearing a sleeveless blouse with a plunging neckline showing more than just a glimpse of her cleavage. He caressed her neck and smelled her body with an intention to peep a bit more deep.

"What do you want to see?"

"Me?…Nothing," he stuttered, redfaced.

Her lips looked enticing as she kept on looking at him with her big black eyes. He moved forward to kiss her and she didn't resist. Their lips met. The intensity was unbearable. His hand moved uphill from her navel. She held her hand just before it reached her curves. He tried to manoeuvre by kissing her more passionately but she remained firm. He moved from her lips to the back of her neck. She closed her eyes, her head thrown back in fervour. He again thought of giving a shot to feel her hills, but she threw his hand aside. He looked at her surprised.

"Go home. I have some work," Sheena said, getting up to quash all his longings within a second.

"But…why…what happened?" he fumbled.

"Nothing, I just want to be left alone," Sheena said with the final signal to Pratyush to leave her apartment.

Her face was closed as a vault. He felt dejected after losing yet another battle to her.

A know-it-all smile came to her face. She loved the feeling of winning such duels.

◦◦◦

Vimarsh was staring at the ceiling. The rotating fan was in turn staring at him, giving him a glimpse of his life so far…moving, but going nowhere.

He looked at his phone. There were no missed calls or even a single forwarding message.

He again stared at the ceiling.

His parents' death in a car accident, six years ago, had left his present in a devastating harmony with his past.

His nearest relative was now his flat-mate, Nikhil aka Nick.

He pressed some buttons on his cell.

"Please press 1 for Hindi, press 2 for Kannada, press 3 for English," a computerised voice echoed in the room.

He pressed 3.

"Please press 1 for blah services, press 2 for blah blah services, press 3 for blah blah blah services or press 4 for speaking to our customer executive."

Key 4 was pressed instantly.

"All our customer executives are busy. Please remain on line. Your call is important to us." The usual friendly voice greeted Vimarsh followed by a melancholy tune.

Vimarsh looked at the time…it was already five minutes and still no response from the other side, with the same tune blaring again and again.

"Hello sir, welcome to BlahalB Teleservices. How can I help you?"

"Actually I don't know how to say this…are you free?" Vimarsh hesitatingly asked.

"Sir, if you want to know about our new schemes, I can explain them to you now," the voice at the other end said, gauging his hesitation.

"Actually yes! I would really like to know about it."

The voice then explained various parameters and features of their new schemes.

"…So sir, would you like me to activate it for your cell?"

"Yeah, okay. That will be good."

"Okay sir, it will be activated in a few minutes. Anything else that you want me to do?"

"Actually I thought if you are free, then can you talk to me for a while? I am quite alone in my life and I want to share my sentiments and emotions with someone," Vimarsh finally said.

"Sorry sir, but I don't understand," the voice at the other end sounded more shocked than helpful.

"No, don't get me wrong. Actually I am very lonely in life and I wanted to talk to someone about it. I hope we can talk sometime. You can also tell me about your feelings, I will be glad to know about them."

"Sir, if you have any other queries regarding any of our services, I would be happy to help you," the voice said, still sounding unsure about why he was not hanging up the phone.

"I will take all the plans you have, but don't hang up…please."

In a split second, the mass between the two ears, at the other end, processed this critical piece of information. The response was rather quick, "Sir, we have many good schemes just for our esteemed customers like you." The voice sounded more enthusiastic now.

"My boss hates me…no, in fact I hate him more," Vimarsh said, now ranting.

"Yes sir, we have a scheme just for the same purpose. Do you want me to tell you about it?"

"I always thought that once I started earning, I would be able to lead my life as I want – just like an independent guy."

"So sir, do you want this scheme in your cell phone?"

"Yes…I am independent…"

"Thank you, sir. It will only take a few moments."

"…But I am not happy. Are you happy?"

"Yes sir, I am. Sir we have another scheme suited for this particular need of yours. Would you like me to activate it for you?"

"It is good that…"

"Thank you, sir. This will take a few moments. Kindly hold on."

"…You are happy. You are so lucky to be happy. Well everyone is happy and lucky except me," Vimarsh said, thinking about himself.

"VIMARSH WHOM ARE YOU TALKING TO?"

"Hey, I have to go. Will talk to you later. Thanks for listening," Vimarsh said, looking at the door.

Vimarsh put the cell by his side and again started looking at the ceiling, with his mind fixed on the person behind the door.

The door creaked open.

"Who were you talking to?" Nick asked, entering the room.

"Nobody," Vimarsh stammered.

"Again those fuckin customer-care executives?" Nick laughed loudly. Vimarsh said nothing.

"Why don't you fuckin understand that they are not your fuckin well-wishers? They only use idiots like you," Nick said, getting hysterical.

Vimarsh looked sideways. He wanted to end this conversation as soon as possible.

"Why don't you fuckin tell me if you have any problems? I am your fuckin friend, God dammit."

"I don't have any problems," Vimarsh said meekly.

"It's that fuckin Vishvesh again."

"Yes, sort of."

"Why don't you kick his fuckin ass instead of kissing it? You might get some fuckin bonus points from my side at least."

"I don't kiss his ass. I am not that kind of a person. I don't want any bonus points also," Vimarsh said, looking for ways to run away from him and from the room.

"Anyway, leave all this. You know that I lost my fuckin credit card."

"I do have mine with me, right now."

"You got yours from the bank?"

"Why don't you take mine?" Vimarsh offered timidly.

"What did you just say?"

"I didn't mean that, but if you need, you can use mine," Vimarsh repeated again with more force although the tone was quite docile this time.

"Don't kid with your fuckin daddy. Okay? I will take it but only this time. I am already getting late. Where is it?" Nick asked, getting restless.

"It is there in my wallet," Vimarsh said, smilingly.

"Thanks, dude. We are best friends."

"Yes, we are, dude. Bestest friends," Vimarsh said joyously.

But no conversation of this sort actually happened. Since it is my suicide note, I think I should write only the truth even if it is about my BESTEST FRIEND. So here it is what actually happened.

"…You are happy. You are so lucky to be happy. Well, everyone is happy and lucky except me," Vimarsh said, thinking about himself.

"VIMARSH, WHOM ARE YOU TALKING TO?"

"Hey, I have to go. Will talk to you later. Thanks for listening," Vimarsh said, looking at the door.

Vimarsh put the cell by his side and again started looking at the ceiling with his mind fixed on the person behind the door.

The door creaked open.

"Who were you talking to?" Nick asked, entering the room.

"Nobody," Vimarsh stammered.

"Again those fuckin customer-care executives?" Nick laughed loudly. Vimarsh said nothing.

"When will you fuckin understand that they are not your fuckin well-wishers? They only use LOSERS like you and make MONEY," Nick said, getting hysterical. Vimarsh glanced sideways. He wanted to end this conversation as soon as possible.

"Why don't you fuckin tell me if you have extra money to spend? I am your fuckin friend, goddammit. I would love to have your extra money. Why waste it on services which you don't need?"

"I don't have any extra money or problems," Vimarsh said meekly.

"It's that fuckin Vishvesh again. Oh poor Vim bar…you are such a fuckin loser. Did he again scare you with his lovely antics? I just love that guy."

"No, nothing of that sort happened."

"Why don't you kiss his fuckin ass instead of crying on your pillow? You might get some fuckin bonus points for this social service."

"I can't kiss his ass. I am not that kind of a person. I don't want any bonus points either," Vimarsh said, still looking for ways to run away from him and from the room.

"You don't or you can't. Anyways, leave all this. I need your fuckin credit card."

"I don't have it right now."

"You lost it again?"

"I don't want to give it to you," Vimarsh said forcefully.

"What did you just say?"

"I don't want to give it to you," Vimarsh repeated again with more force, though the tone was quite docile this time,

"Don't kid with your daddy. I am getting late. Where is it?" Nick was getting restless.

Vimarsh looked helplessly around but the flat was the adobe of only two tenants.

"Where is it?"

"In my wallet."

"Thanks, dude. You are my fuckin best friend."

"Yes, we are, dude. Bestest friends," Vimarsh said sarcastically.

10

"Are you going to office?" Vimarsh asked.

"Yes sissy. What do you expect me to do on a fuckin Wednesday?"

"Can you drop me? I am already getting late," Vimarsh pleaded.

Nick looked at him with disgust in his eyes. "You have five hundred bucks?"

"Yes...why?" Vimarsh at once regretted asking for a favour.

"This fuckin bike needs petrol just like you need hay for food."

"But why don't you get it filled with fuel?"

"Because my dearest fuckin retard friend, this is your bike and it is your moral responsibility."

"Then why do you drive it?"

"So, now you want to drive it? Okay, go on." Nick at once moved away from the bike.

Vimarsh looked at the bustling traffic outside and looked at the 180cc machine standing beside him.

"What happened dude? *Phat gayi*?"

"I will take a bus," Vimarsh said.

"If you have five hundred bucks, I would love to drop you...may be in some fuckin garbage can."

Vimarsh said nothing.

"Okay, sit, but this is the last time I am droping you anywhere."

Vimarsh said nothing. Quietly obeyed. The insult was less painful than reaching office late.

༄

"Here it is, your lovely second home," Nick said, stopping at the gate of AKFC. "Hey, who is that pretty bitch?"

"I don't know," Vimarsh said, not wanting to create a scene in front of his office. "Don't talk like that here. I work here."

"Oh yeah, I forgot you are a slave here. But without this little piece of information, I am not going anywhere," Nick said, still looking in the same direction.

"Sheena...her name is Sheena."

"So you do know her. Then why were you hiding it from your daddy? Intro...I need an intro."

"I don't talk to her."

"You don't talk to her! I think the reverse would be more appropriate...moreover, I am not asking you to talk to her. After the intro, you can go to your fuckin office."

"I said we have never talked and don't create a scene here."

"Me...creating a scene here? What are you saying, bro? We are bros, right? How can I get you insulted in front of your own office? Okay, I am going," Nick said and left.

❧

"Hi, bro," the bike screeched loudly before halting in front of Vimarsh. "Going home? Same here. Why don't you take a lift on your own bike?"

Vimarsh looked at him suspiciously.

"Hey, there she is," Nick added.

"Are you going to get her introduced to me or not?" Nick waited for an answer but Sheena was moving very fast and so was the time.

❧

"Hi...," silence stretched itself in between.

Sheena looked taken aback at the greeting from an unknown source.

"...I am Nick...I mean Nikhil."

"Do I know you?" she asked, still confused.

"I am Vimarsh's friend," Nick said boldly.

Sheena still looked perplexed.

"You know Vimarsh...right?"

"No."

"I mean…he works in your office."

"There are more than four hundred people in my office. And even if I was familiar with this name, still I would like to know the reason for YOU stalking me?"

"Nothing…sorry…ma'am."

"Where are you going?"

"Nothing…I am really sorry."

"Where are you going?"

"Domlur."

"I am also going in the same direction. Drop me near the flyover," Sheena said, moving towards the bike.

Nick didn't know what to take from the unexpected turn of events. He kick started the bike.

Vimarsh, who was standing at a distance, unaware of their conversation, looked astounded as the bike zoomed off, leaving a trail of dust.

༺ଓ༻

"Stop there," Sheena said, pointing her finger from behind his back.

"So, if in case you want to go anywhere tonight or some other night, you can give me a call," Nick said as a parting statement.

"Why at night only? You don't provide services in daytime?"

"No, it is not that but mostly I am free at night."

"Okay, will think about it."

"Okay…so I should go now," Nick asked, without making a move to go.

"Wait…," Sheena said.

Nick looked at her like an expectant mother looking at her doctor.

A loud sound attracted the attention of every passerby present nearby.

"Why?"

"For stalking me."

"But I wasn't stalking you."

"Okay then, that was for ogling at the wrong places."

Nick said nothing.

"It would be better, if you were to leave now."

Everyone was looking at him with disgust. At a public place, messing with a woman was not a good idea, not even slightly. He started the bike's engine, trying to look comfortable in a difficult situation. Sheena smiled, as Nick's bike zoomed away.

〜◎〜

"What happened?" Vimarsh asked as soon as Nick entered.

"Nothing, I floored her totally."

"SHE SLAPPED YOU."

"Slap…and me? Never ever a fuckin possibility, bro."

"What about those marks on your face?"

"That fuckin bike fell on me."

"On your face?"

"Not on my face…how can you be so fuckin idiot? I am going to my room."

〜◎〜

"Excuse me…are you Vimarsh?"

"Ye…yes…yes," Vimarsh stammered.

"Yesterday it was your friend who was stalking me?"

"I am s…s…sorry…," Vimarsh said, still stammering.

"What do you mean by sorry?" Sheena flared. "Have you looked at yourself or your friend?" Sheena asked, definitely not joking as everyone stood, looking at Vimarsh's desk. The scene concluded in just over five minutes. The longest and unforgettable five minutes of his life.

Vimarsh left office early that day. The insult was too hard to let go and his mere helplessness was making him hate his life more than ever.

11

Today 00:30 a.m.

"Twelve…thirteen…fourteen…fifteen…

But you know what?…Sheena is also not the primary reason for my suicide. The reason for my suicide is far more deep than you can ever imagine. WHY? You are asking why?…Then listen, it is because I love her. I love her from the core of my heart and today I will prove that by sacrificing my life for her. But before that, I want to tell this world about her, since she deserves that much recognition in my suicide note."

Part III
The Angel

12

Six years ago

"Hi…I am wanting to be friends with you," stuttered a boy in front of her.

"Hello…I am your senior. Would you want me to take you somewhere?" said another, kneeling down.

Next day

"No sir, I didn't mean that…she is like my sister, sir…never in my life will I look at her with any other intention. *Sachchi* sir…by God *ki kasam* sir…Sir, that *dhondu* is also trying to propose to her since so many days…okay, sir I will warn him sir, on your behalf. Don't worry sir, she is yours. No one will look at her," said the guy, knelt down again, in front of a burly senior of his college.

Many tried to hold her forever in their arms but she always managed to escape. She loved them, teased them, eluded them and finally left them at her will, sometimes without giving a single word of explanation. In school she always received attention from the boys, sometimes wontedly but mostly unwanted. As she progressed towards her graduation years, this attention became a normal part of her life and as to when she became addicted to it, she could never tell.

Then came the proposals…first from the seniors and then from her batch-mates. She still fondly remembers holding the record for getting the most number of roses on the Rose Day for four consecutive years of her graduation.

Then arrived the fashion show, where she represented her college in a national level festival at one of the leading colleges of the country. Those five days were one of the most treasured moments of her life. She received twenty-three proposals in those five days and the icing on the cake was the third place in the overall rankings as the best participant in the fest. The main attraction was that the guys, who were at the top two positions, had already expressed their love for her through letters and flowers. So, in a way, she was at the top.

After joining her job, she found herself in the garden city, Bangalore. First day itself in the office brought an unexpected turn in her life when she found a young man of age around twenty-eight, sitting next to her. Instantly she was smitten with his looks and personality.

After thinking of numerous ways to impress him, she was truly astonished when one day he asked her out for dinner in the most regal manner any girl could ever dream of. And her response was a big YES. And that night, the dinner started a series of conversations (both online and offline). Meetings after office hours and movies and shopping on weekends became a normal routine.

He told her that he had liked her from the moment he had laid his eyes on her. Made her more secure about her allure. No man in this world could say 'no' to her inviting eyes, she proclaimed this to herself, looking at her own reflection in the mirror, that night.

Anchit truly was the man of her dreams or she assumed him to be one.

13

One-and-a-half months ago

"One ticket for ITPL," a soft voice startled Vimarsh in the bus.

A girl in a yellow floral suit was standing at the gate.
Where are you from? I love you.
I love you, my sweetheart.
Accept me as your slave.
Vimarsh could hear all kinds of thoughts flowing in the bus for her. Longings and desires.
Vimarsh felt a ting in his heart.

⚜

"Are you not coming?"
   "Where?"
   "KMA meetings…didn't you get the mail?"
   "KMA meetings?" Vimarsh asked.
   "Do you even work here? You are asking what KMA meetings are?"
   "Is it about any new policy of the company?" Vimarsh asked as his intellect warned him to resolve this issue before entering the conference room. But he received only a mocking laughter in return.
   The conference room was still half empty.
   People present there were seated in the far corner from the seat on which Vishvesh was to sit, but he had yet not arrived. And no one was eager to become another scapegoat like…? Like Vimarsh and who else?
   Vishvesh arrived almost thirty minutes later.
   "Hau aar you pee-pul?" The question echoed in the room.
   "Fine sir…we are fine…yeah, yeah, we are fine, sir," echoed many voices at once.
   "So what izz going aan?"
   "Work as usual sir," Sankat replied, when no one else said anything. He dodged some nasty stares from the rest of the crowd.
   "Good…good. Naarmally pee-pul here are spend their time in spreading gaasips. It is good that somebody is giving prior to wok aalso," Vishvesh proclaimed in his Cambridge-certified lingo.
   Sankat blushed; Vimarsh bit his lips.
   "We are having these interact once a week, to know the praagress of the wok and aalso appreciate those who are doing good wok and if

yenyoñe are yeny concerns you can talk about it here. Ass yeveryone knows we follow open door paalicy. You peepul is our most valuable resources."

"That is a good idea, sir," remarked someone, flashing a smile while seconding the idea.

"Absolutely sir, it is a very innovative idea. I don't think anyone ever thought of this in any other company," another added.

"Sir, you are such a genius," Sankat added earnestly.

"I know you are appreciate this idea." Vishvesh revealed his white teeth, till now lying hidden behind his bushy moustache. "I are called this mating for a some very impaartant issues. Javier sir is called me to discuss very impaartant discussion. It is but aabvious that who else they kaal to discuss that kind of impaartant discussion," he laughed at his own joke. Others joined in as if they were drowning and only by laughing at his joke could they protect their souls.

"You are right, sir...who else Javier sir will summon?" someone else jumped in the fray.

Vishvesh cleared his throat as if announcing the Nobel Peace prize of the year. "The manaegement feels that some of the emplaayees are develop a sense of 'home' in their little kabicals (cubicals). The manaegement fears that soon a sense of aawnership (ownership) will set in peepul's mind which are turn into *over self esteemed attitudes* and the result: *Good bye* to productivity. So the manaegement are decide to assign the kabicles on the basis of first come first serve. No one will have a permanent wok space and hence no unproductive homey feelings are comes into picture and become a showstaapper for us."

"What an innovative concept, sir!" Sanket applauded Vishvesh. Others joined him with a smile on their faces.

It sounded more like a public toilet kind of arrangement to Vimarsh.

Vishvesh continued with his management theologies, "As you aal are well known that the company laast year decided to remove the kaancept of raeise and introduce the kaancept of bonuses, if five out of yeight company goals are met. I are personally very sad to announce that since only four out of yeight goals are met last year, so no bonuses to yenyone, this year."

A bolt from the blue for everyone; even for Sankat. "Sir, what were the goals that we missed?" Vimarsh asked sarcastically.

"You can come in my kaabin if you waant to know about it."

"Sir, we have an open door policy and I think everyone here wants to know the same."

Vishvesh looked at the rest of the crowd but everyone was curious to know the four reasons which were responsible for losing their bonuses.

"Aukay, the goals we missed are cushtomer service improvement goal, praaductivity enhaancement goal, is-tream-line praacesses faar maximising praapensities goal and EMPLAAYEE MORALE."

"Excuse me, but what was the last goal?"

"Emplaayee morale."

There was no response from anyone once Vishvesh finished with his explanations. Sensing it as a signal to move forward, he continued with the next policy change, "Lately, our aafice is witnessing a laat of thefts so aafter laat of consideration and some out of the baax thinking emplaayed by Javier sir, a major decision are taken by the manaegement to introduce two new prograams.

- A random emplaayee search prograam.
- An 'emplaayee dignity enhancement' prograam.'

Everyone looked amused.

"I know you peepul are happy that our manaegement thinks so much about its emplaayees. In addition to this, the company laptaaps which are provide to each emplaayee are aalso feared to be stolen hence aal the laptaaps will be paarmanently attached to the emplaayees' desk."

"But sir, the laptops were given to us to use while travelling." Vimarsh interrupted, unable to control himself now.

"Will you take respaansibility if any theft takes place in the future?"

Vimarsh looked at Vishvesh with what-an-idiot expression, but said nothing. Vishvesh continued looking slightly perturbed at Vimarsh's constant questioning about the sacred management decisions, but he nevertheless continued, "The manaegement, last year, decided to start an emplaayee recognation prograam, where the besht emplaayee aaf the year are visited by a man dressed as a taartaaise and give him a five hundred worth of gift vaucher, a pen and a certificate of excellence. I are sorry to infaarm you that after careful and long discussion, the prograam are scrapped becaase we couldn't find yenyone who could fill in the role of a taartaaise. I know you peepul are disappointed but we will think of something new soon."

Was it a warning or a signal of the imminent bad days, nobody could tell?

"Now the most impaartant manaegement news of today, faar which this mating has been caaled. The is adding a new designate of a manager for finance and administration in this aafice. Javier sir is entrust this respaansibility on my broad shoulders." Vimarsh looked at his fat bulges below his large ears. They looked more like cowdung than shoulders, "I are nominate some names for this post. In the next six months they are evaluate in various parameters. After that Javier sir and I will decide the best caendidate," Vishvesh said, clearing his throat. At this point, he was clearly not eager to stretch the meeting any longer. "Simbu S., Gautam Reddy, Sheena and Sankat. These are the four names."

Surprises.

"Very good decision, sir," finally one of the untouched lot said, hiding his anger and disappointment behind the veil of a smile.

"Yes sir, very well chosen, sir."

"The new manager needs to *centralise* our resources to make them more efficient."

"Sir, you are a management genius."

Vimarsh recalled a memo which he had received a year ago: "We need to *decentralise* our systems to remove the complacencies."

Vimarsh was hurt at seeing his name omitted from the list but he could finally find the answer to the purpose of KMA meetings.

Kiss My Ass meetings.

14

"I love you."

"What?"

"I love you," Vimarsh said as everyone looked at him with amazement in the packed bus.

Obviously, proposing to a girl and that too in a bus, by any means, was not a conventional approach.

"Do I know you?"

"Not yet but you will…soon. Anyways, I am Vimarsh."

"I am…"

"You are my dream girl, I know…and I also know a few more things about you."

Some more exchanged glances in the bus. The world is really short of beautiful single girls.

"About me? Like what?" she asked, surprisingly pleased.

"Like you wore a pink floral suit yesterday and also on last to last Thursday. You wear light colours, especially white, on Mondays, red or orange on Tuesday…"

She was looking rather impressed,

"…On Wednesdays you prefer to wear cream coloured suits and Thursdays are reserved for yellow, mustard or light brown. Also, you have two watches out of which you mostly wear the one with the black strap and golden dial and you always keep a water bottle and an umbrella with you."

"Have you done some kind of research on me? I mean this is incredible. I never thought that someone would find me worthy of so much interest."

"I know people are so blind and even if they do like someone, I mean even if they are really fond of a pretty girl, they hesitate to express their feelings. What is so difficult in conveying your feelings to someone? We both are human beings and human beings have feelings."

"You are so right," she seemed excited.

"I knew you are not like one of those close minded people but feel it is perfectly okay to have feelings for someone you really like or admire."

"I just wish that everyone could start thinking like you."

"You bet, but there is only one more person like me."

"Who?"

"The man I see daily in the mirror."

"You are so funny," she laughed loudly.

Vimarsh smiled. Finally he had nailed the final frontier.

"Big Bazaar Stop," the conductor shouted near his face.

Vimarsh saw her laugh, standing at a safe distance from him. He looked around and saw the software workers of various MNCs rubbing their bodies against each other in their steel cage. He looked at her longingly as she again laughed at some silly jokes of her friend.

The dream was much better, he thought and got off the bus.

~❦~

"Vimarsh…Vimarsh…get up," Nick weakly shook Vimarsh from his sleep.

"What happened?" Vimarsh asked, greatly irritated at being woken up at such an odd hour.

"Can't you see that I am sick?" Nick coughed.

"No, you are not."

"How can you be so heartless, Vimarsh? Your best friend is swinging between life and death and you are not even asking him to rest."

"Okay, take some rest Nick. In the morning we'll go to the doctor."

"Morning? Are you insane, Vimarsh? Here I am so critical and you want to wait till the morning to consult a fuckin doctor?"

"So, what do you want me to do?"

"Do something…I don't know…I am sick…I can't think."

"Okay, go to your room. I'll think of something."

"I can't go in my room on my own…I am sick…Take me to my room or let me sleep here."

"How did you come here?"

"I was less ill at that time."

"Okay, let's go," Vimarsh relented, knowing there was no point in arguing with Nick at such a juncture. His past experiences had told him to keep his trap shut at such moments. He was only worried whether he would be able to go to office in the morning or not.

"Take this."

"What is this?"

"This is a cough syrup."

"You don't understand, I am terribly sick and this minor medication won't help me."

"I know Nick, but we don't have any other alternative in the middle of the night. It will keep you alive till morning, and then we will go to the doctor."

"Okay."

"Good boy."

"Vimarsh, I don't wan'na die."

"You won't die. Now drink this."

"Okay," Nick gulped the syrup.

"Now take some rest. It will do you good."

"Where are you going?" Nick muttered.

"I am here only; in the adjacent room."

"No, no, please don't go. Stay here."

"I am here only Nick, right across the hall. Don't worry. I will come after every one hour to check on you."

"One hour is too long."

"Okay, I will come in every half hour."

"Half hour?"

"NICK."

"Please don't shout. I am dying here…half hour is fine."

"Good boy."

❧❧

"Vimarsh…Vimarsh…Vimarsh."

"What happened now?" Vimarsh was now almost fuming.

"It has been thirty-five minutes and you didn't come to see me."

15

"Where izz that idiot?" Vishvesh.

"That idiot!" somebody exclaimed. "Who is *that idiot*?" but in whispers.

"He is talking about Vimarsh," Sankat clarified in the same whispering tone.

"Will somebody say me where izz that IDIOT?" Vishvesh roared again, standing outside his cabin.

"Sir, he has yet not arrived," Samy said feebly.

"Is he call or inform to anyone?"

No one said anything.

"When he comes…aask him to meet me."

"Hello sir." Vimarsh was on the phone.

"Who is this?"

"Sir, this is me…Vimarsh."

"Veemars!" Vishvesh tried to remember the name for some time.

"Sir, actually my flat-mate is very ill, so I will be a bit late to office."

Exactly at that particular moment it hit Vishvesh. "No no, today there is very impaartant mating with Javier sir. Javier sir is coming here. Everyone should be present in the aafice when he comes. You need to be here. Since he is coming you need to be here. He comes here and no one is here then he will feel very bad. No, no, this should naat be the case," he said in one breath.

"But sir, my flat-mate…"

"I do naat want to hear yeny silly reasons. Come aafice soon. Soon mean SOON." Vishvesh roared on the phone.

"But sir…"

"Am I naat clear Mishter Veemars?"

"Yes sir."

"GOOD."

᠁ঔ৩ঔ᠁

"Nick I have to go to office."

Nick had already been looking at Vimarsh talking with his boss.

"So are you gon'na leave your best friend to die here to attend your fuckin office?"

"It is urgent."

"Urgent than your friend's funeral?"

"Nick, if you behave properly and take rest, I will get you a chocolate."

"Only a chocolate?"

"Okay two, but not more than that."

"Dairy Milk…big one."

"Okay, now take rest and I will be back soon."

᠁ঔ৩ঔ᠁

Vimarsh entered his office.

"Boss has called you," Samy informed him at the gate.

"May I come in, sir?"

"Who is this idiot who doesn't even know when to come into my kaebin?" Vishvesh shouted.

Vimarsh slowly backed off, closing the door.

"Come in. Who is it?" Vishvesh asked, opening the door to look out for the offender, "Oh, I should heb knew, it could be no one yelse."

"Sorry, sir."

"No, no, I are sorry sir," Vishvesh said in an acerbic tone. "Please sir, come inside sir, please sir, I inshisht," he promptly moved aside.

Vimarsh had no other option except to comply.

Javier was sitting at the far end, looking eagerly for the person who was at the receiving end.

"Yes sir, what can I do faar you?" Vishvesh asked, closing the door behind him.

"You had called me sir," Vimarsh mumbled, trying not to look at Javier who was looking at the file of Krystal Kare which Vimarsh had prepared a few days back (or a few nights back).

"Oh yeah, yeah, so you are free nau to visit this smoll office? Javier sir, I are telling about the low IQ guy, he is the one. Sir, we are totally faallow our company paalicy. Everyone is equal and should be treat like equals. Sir, we have peepul like Sankat on one hand who are the back bone of this affice and then on the other side we have peepul like...you know what I are saying," Vishvesh said forcefully, putting his point forward. Javier seemed least bit interested.

"We need peepul like Sankat at the top so that they can take care of this company as their own companies."

Vimarsh wanted to get out from the room a.s.a.p. but couldn't.

"You...yeah, you...fraam nau aan you are help Sankat in administration."

"Sir, but..."

"I know it izz diffu-cult faar you but Sankat will guide you and do naat worry, you are aalso learn yeverything soon," Vishvesh said, looking at him with glee.

Vimarsh hated that look instantly.

"Okay Vishvesh, I got your point. Let Sankat manage the administration for some time; then we will see."

"Okay, Veemars you can go nau."

He came out without saying anything. He was trembling violently with shame and rage. People looked at him for a moment, only to disregard him completely.

"Sankat sir, Vishvesh sir is calling you inside his office," he heard Samy inform Sankat.

⤳◯⤲

Vimarsh saw her again but this time he had company.

"Hey, Vimarsh where are you going?"

"Office. Why?"

"Let me drop you…till the fuckin bus stop," Nick said, laughing, on his own joke.

"No, it's okay."

Nick tried to start the bike but it refused to budge from its place.

"I am coming with you," he said, when even after a few more attempts, the bike failed to start.

Vimarsh clenched his fists.

"Be happy, my best friend, we are not going to office together for the first time…so don't panic," Nick was obviously happy. "Hey, who is she?"

Vimarsh looked at the direction and the reason for which he didn't want Nick to come with him was standing right in front of them.

ᵔ⊙ᵔ

"I am in love with her," Nick expressed his love for her.

Vimarsh clenched his teeth. "She is out of your league," he said.

"What do you fuckin know about my league?"

"I know everything."

"I don't need your fuckin advice," Nick snapped.

ᵔ⊙ᵔ

"I love her."

"Whom?" Nick looked at Vimarsh with annoyance.

"That girl you were ogling at today morning."

"Do you even know her fuckin name?"

"That's none of you business. And don't use *that word* for her."

"It is still an open field. Anybody can win and we both know who will win."

"I love her."

"I heard that already. Go fuck yourself and let me sleep," Nick said.

16

Today 00:55 a.m.

'Finally, it is time to say goodbye to all who would read this suicide note…sixteen…seventeen…eighteen…crap…finished…only eighteen pills so far before I wish adieu at this crucial time of my life.'

He opened the door to get some more.

The darkness screeched silently to give way to brightness from the room, which got lit when the lights of the hall were switched on. They beamed at him with relief.

The door across the hall was closed. A thin ray of light crept in from the space between the door and the floor.

'What is he doing at this time of the night?' he wondered.

17

"Vimarsh, open the fuckin door. I know you are awake, not fuckin sleeping. OPEN THE DAMN DOOR," Nick shouted in the semi-dark hallway.

The silence expanded itself again, once the banging stopped. No attempt from the other side was made to change the moment's stillness.

"VIMARSH…"

No one replied.

"VIMARSH…OPEN THE FUCKIN DOOR…I DON'T LIKE THIS KIND OF CRAP," Nick shouted, though his face contorted with lines of worry visible all over it.

"MR REDDY, OPEN THE DOOR…PLEASE," he begged now. The word please came a little late but the thumping nevertheless continued.

"WHAT HAPPENED…NICK?" Mr Reddy, their neighbour was definitely looking dishevelled on being woken up so late at night.

"It's Vimarsh…he is not opening the door. Can you please come?" begged Nick. Mr Reddy was now looking irritated and worried at the same time.

⟶◎⟵

The clock struck eleven with a soft sound.

Vimarsh lay on the bed, while Nick sat beside him, reading a newspaper.

"Who brought me here?" Vimarsh asked delicately, expecting a sarcastic reply.

"You swallowed 43 pills in one shot…fuckin extraordinaire," but didn't get one.

"Why did you save me?" He continued with his slim odds.

"If you really want to know…okay…I don't want any fuckin legal headaches because of your failed suicide attempts in our flat. And you owe me five thousand fuckin bucks for keeping your idiocy out of the police records," Nick smiled, "Next time try to use a building or a bridge to demonstrate your fuckin wisdom."

Vimarsh felt each word from Nick biting deep into his skin.

"Hello Mr Vimarsh, I am glad Nick brought you here ON TIME. How are you feeling now?" the doctor asked, as soon as he entered the room.

Vimarsh felt a sudden urge to strangle Nick till his eyeballs popped out of their sockets.

"Thanks Shiva for all the help at the right time and keeping this case out of bounds for the police," Nick said, looking genuinely grateful.

Vimarsh was surprised to discover some new emotions in Nick's wallet of emoticons.

"Shiva and I are college friends. I never knew he was working in this hospital until yesterday when I saw his fuckin name on the doctors' list."

"You have not changed even a bit," Shiva smiled.

"Excuse me, doctor," a nurse interrupted their small talk.

৯৩৫৫৫৯

"Vimarsh, who else is there in your family?"

"No one. My parents died in a car accident six years ago. And after that, I have had no connection with any of my relatives."

"So, your family only consists of Nick."

Vimarsh said nothing.

"What happened? Is anything wrong?" Nick asked.

"Nick…I don't know how to say it?"

"What's happened doctor?" Vimarsh asked, looking real worried.

"Actually Vimarsh, your blood test report has something, I mean… something…which was unexpected."

"Doctor, can you stop posing these riddles and tell me what the matter is exactly?"

"Vimarsh, there is a kind of blood contamination. Normally this happens due to prolonged radiation, but in your case we are not sure how you got affected."

"Is it serious? I mean it is incurable…right?"

"There is no need to worry. We are seeking a second opinion from the specialists in Mumbai. Did you ever face any temporary vision blackouts with excruciating headaches or stomachaches?"

"Yeah, sometimes it did happen but lately the frequency has increased. I think it is because I work on my laptop continuously for long hours. But that could not be the reason…right?"

"Vimarsh, when the battery of the laptop is considerably aged, it starts emitting a certain kind of radiation. But we are not sure that this is the reason. There can be various other reasons too."

"But it is curable, right?"

"Yes, it is curable if detected early. In the worst case, even blood transfusion doesn't work. One can then only hope of surviving to a maximum of four to five months."

"You mean I have only four months to live?"

"I didn't mean that. I was only telling you about the worst case," Shiva said, caught suddenly on the back foot.

"Life has never been fair to me. Now I only have four months to live. I always knew this and now I am going to die," Vimarsh said, beginning to cry loudly.

"Stop crying like a fuckin baby. Nothing is gon'na happen to you," Nick said, finally opening his mouth but looking absolutely shellshocked at the sudden turn of events.

18

God, life is so complicated. I thought faking my suicide would evoke feelings of sacrifice in my best friend's heart and he would sacrifice his so-called love for that girl.

I am no scoundrel and, of course, I love her and have you visualised how Vimarsh and that angel would look together?

She is a diva and he is like a fuckin ogre. No one in his fuckin normal state would want another Shrek. I agree that I am also not some fuckin prince but at least I am no ogre. But things went haywire. Previously we only had a unique, always whining Vimarsh and now we have a unique, dying and always-whining Vimarsh.

"Will you stop crying?" Nick said for the seventh time.

Vimarsh looked at him with hatred oozing out of his red eyes.

"What did I do now? Had I not saved you then, you would have been fuckin happy, I guess."

Vimarsh said nothing.

"Eat this." Nick almost shoved the burger wrapped into a paper into his mouth.

"Get off me."

"Okay, then have this fuckin newspaper. At least give something to your fuckin mind."

"I don't need your help. Thanks a lot."

"As you say, my fuckin best friend," Nick said and left the room.

Vimarsh threw down the paper, in which the burger was wrapped and lay down again to attend to his favourite pastime, looking at the ceiling.

The paper ruffled.

Vimarsh looked for the source but the paper moved beneath the sofa, hiding itself from him.

After a few failed attempts, he finally closed his eyes in desperation.

The paper ruffled again, mocking him.

He finally got up from the sofa and caught hold of its collar. The paper looked at him with shrinking, watery eyes. Vimarsh found his own shadow on the paper wincing with pain. He swiftly straightened the paper.

I can change your entire life…

He smoothened out the rest of the paper.

In SEVEN Days, **Success Guru Proclaims**' – the headline screamed.

"Chris Mohan, a highly recommended success coach by many individuals and companies alike, has claimed that he can turn around anyone's life in seven days. The claim was…"

The paper was torn from the side.

Who is this guy? Strange name…and how can he claim something preposterous like this?

The name Chris Mohan gave at least a million results on Google in no time. He opened a few, including the official site and read the whole thing in a jiffy.

Finally, he opened the 'Contact Us' page.

Part IV
Chris Mohan

19

Born and brought up in a slum. Father was a small-time pickpocket and later a drug peddler. The son was completely unaware about his father's real profession until he heard the news that he had departed forever to meet his creator during a trip to the police custody.

Mother, a prostitute at night and a church-monger in broad daylight, succumbed to the pressures of life when he was fourteen-years old. And hence the son was devoid of both his creators before he could cross fifteen.

His father, when alive, used to come home late. So he paid his debts, for being born as his son, to him by getting beaten black and blue every single day of his childhood. '*You are a born failure. You will never ever be of anything worth,*' was his favourite rap during that whole exercise.

He was always confused that why he was always at the receiving end? Why did his father hate him so much? He finally concluded that if he amounted to nothing in his formative years, his father might start loving him.

After he was left to feed for himself, he tried to steal a piece of bread from a rich kid and was beaten almost to death.

That day he had a profound realisation – the only way to breathe was to breathe like the moneyed. He started with stealing small-time car parts. The big moment arrived when someone handed him ten thousand bucks to deliver a small packet of white powder. And that marked the beginning. He loved the new diversion since it did not involve any violence and produced quick bucks in the backyard.

But it all had to end one day – the day which he could never forget.

He was languishing in a dark, dingy, mosquito-infested cell in his torn pants and oversized half-sleeve shirt. A sub-inspector came inside the cell at almost midnight. He never expected any *uniformwala* to justify his acts.

"I am letting you lose… Don't think it is because of sympathy or anything. You and others like you think that you are in this situation because of the government or the police or some rich bloke or may be because of your destiny. I am also not going to tell you whether you are right or wrong. Just remember, *'whatever you become in life will only be because of the choices you make and not because of the chances you get.'* Now go."

That was the first and the last time he ever went to jail. The first thing he did next morning was to start looking for a job. Weeks went past in a jiffy but no one seemed interested in keeping a boy with a ripped shirt and torn pants, in their swanky stores.

One day, standing in front of a car showroom and starving since the past three days, he thought of becoming a car salesman. He always liked the pretty boxes on four wheels, rolling all around the city. His dream was to drive one of his own some day.

The store was glossy and shiny with new cars teasing and enticing the bystanders. He went inside, fancying his chances of probably acquiring a white-collared job. Two men were busy working on a new car with its bonnet open.

He went straight to them. "I need a job," he said.

No one looked at him.

"I need a job," he said again.

"*Aye ladke*, how did you come inside? Where the hell is the security…SECURITY, SECURITY!"

A fair-complexioned kid dressed as a guard came running.

"Sorry sir, I went to the latrine. *Aye ladke,* how dare you come inside? Get out now," he roared at the boy.

"Sir, I need some more time to make this car work," the other man, who was still looking at the engine, said. "I still don't know what the problem is."

"I can do it," the boy said, sensing this to be his last chance.

"What can you do? *Ladke,* are you out of your freaking mind?"

"I can do it."

"What if you can't?" the manager asked.

"What if I can?"

"You will get the job," the manager said.

"But sir…," the other guy interrupted.

"Wait Shekhar, I want to see what this half-pants got in there?"

"I need a small hammer."

"God dammit, this is a brand new car," Shekhar said irritatingly.

"A DEFECTIVE brand new car…HAMMER," the boy corrected him.

"Give him one," the manager interrupted.

The boy was soon lost in total concentration. His frail body was leaning on the open front of the car. The car was teasing him like a bloody virgin.

'One day you will be mine,' the boy looked at her longingly.

'In your dreams baby,' she chided him.

'You just wait…you bloody whore,' he replied.

"It's ready," he said, looking at the three pairs of eyes.

"It can't be," the other guy panicked.

"Let me check," the manager took the keys.

The car started with the sound of a sleeping beauty aroused from her sleep. The boy smiled.

"You get the job," the manager announced slowly.

"And three hundred bucks as my payment."

"You have some attitude."

"I prefer to call it guts."

"What is your name?"

"Chris Mohan," the boy thought for a moment before uttering his name. He had never thought about it before but he wanted a new name for a new life. His only God was his mother and since he always saw her going to various shrines, especially churches and temples, he considered his new name an apt testimony to her memory.

"Okay, you will be the mechanic from now on to work under him."

"I can be a better salesman," he said, looking at the salesmen crowding the showroom. His eyes were looking longingly at their smartly creased clothes.

"Are you out of your fucking mind?" Shekhar said impatiently.

"I can do it."

"What if you can't?" the manager retorted.

"What if I can?"

"You have one day to prove your mettle as a salesman. You won't take the floor-time from any other salesman here. If they are all busy with other customers and someone comes from that door, you can only attend to that client."

So he waited longingly in an oversize dress for that first unattended customer.

It was 8:30 and the showroom was about to close. Not many customers had visited the showroom so far. He suddenly saw a feeble, scared-looking man, making his way slowly into the store. The boy waited for other salesmen to approach him but none of them seemed interested in interrupting their leaving-for-home ritual in the middle.

The man looked at the busy salesmen with expectations in his eyes, but none paid him any heed.

"Hello sir, may I help you?" he said finally, approaching his first customer with a trembling heart.

"No…no, I was just looking."

"Sir, there is no need to worry. I will also be worried if I am not able to assist you to see the best cars that we have here," the boy said, looking at the other salesmen from the corner of his eyes. They were still not interested in coming over. His confidence increased; this was his only chance to become like them.

He didn't remember what he said thereafter. The only thing he remembered was that his first customer said 'yes' to a car, relying on his words of wisdom.

In his second month, he sold eighteen cars and this gave him the confidence to breathe lightly. Much to his amazement, the owner of the showroom fired him for being too aggressive. Some of the other salesmen had complained.

At this point, Chris realised he could sell cars. He had proved it to himself and he was ready to prove it to the world – including his deceased father. He soon found employment at another car dealer. Here he worked at what he did better than anyone else – sell automobiles!

For eleven straight years, he sold more new retail cars than any other salesperson in the whole state; more as an individual than most dealers sold in all. No other salesperson had ever retained this title for more than a year.

Lekha, one of his customers, was working in an organisation which provided sales training to big corporate houses. She asked Chris to come and attend one of the seminars as a participant and speak when one of the speakers had withdrawn his name at the last minute.

So he came, he delivered and he rocked!

That night, his eleven years of hardcore experience in sales made him a superstar in front of some eight hundred odd salespersons. He started receiving invites from various parts of the country to make sales presentations and impart training.

In 2006, he wrote his first book about his forte. And some 100,000 copies of it got sold. He then left car dealership for his new passion – training people to sell more, to fight more with the life's roadblocks and of course, writing books.

In 2007, he tied the knot with Lekha.

20

"Sir, I need some days off," Vimarsh stood in Vishvesh's cabin.

"LEAVES YOU MEAN! Why? What leaves? No, no, it izz naat paasible. No leaves till new year."

"Sir, but I have not taken any leave till now this year."

"But you have aalso not done yeny work till nau."

"This time it is urgent. I can't postpone it."

Vishvesh looked at Vimarsh. He appeared resolute. "Aukay, hau many daeys you waant?" he said biting his lips.

"Twenty days."

"TWENTY DAEYS! Naat paasible. Too laang. Take five daeys, that izz the max I can give."

"I am going for twenty days. I can't cancel it," Vimarsh said adamantly.

"Aukay take seven daeys but naat more than that."

"I told you my problem already. I can't take less than that," Vimarsh said confidently, secretly enjoying the duel.

Vishvesh stared at him with bloodshot eyes but Vimarsh stood firm.

"Aukay...apply the leaves and I will approve once they comes with me."

"I don't have enough leave now...will apply once they are credited to my account after this quarter," Vimarsh said with a poker face.

"Hau many you have?"

"Casual leaves, I think, are four; sick leaves are ten and earned leaves are twelve," Vimarsh said.

"So you have enough leaves, what izz the praablem? Apply yearned leaves."

"I don't want to waste my earned leave."

"No, no...why? What izz the praablem?"

"I don't want to apply for my earned ones."

"No, no...why? What izz the praablem?"

"One gets money for unused earned leaves."

"No, no...I didn't get you. Where izz the praablem?"

"I do not want to use them."

"No, no that's aukay but what izz the praablem?" he kept on parroting the same thing.

"I have already told you the reason."

Vishvesh still looked confused about the reason, but, nevertheless chose to change his stance, "Aukay, apply sick leave."

"Sick leave! In advance?"

"Why?"

"One can't apply sick leave in advance. How can I assume that I am going to fall sick next week?"

"No, no…have you ever tried it?"

"There is no point of trying something which is not possible," Vimarsh said, trying hard not to laugh.

"No, no…try it and then let me know…I will approve then."

"Sir, even if I apply in advance, you cannot approve them. Javier sir might ask how you could approve such leave in advance."

"Oh izz it…then wait…do naat apply nau. Let me confirm it with someone."

"Sir, I also wanted to ask you one more thing. I have worked for continuous five weekends. So I was thinking if I will get compensation for them?"

"Compensation off?"

"The one which you get when you work on a holiday," Vimarsh explained.

"Yeah, yeah…don't worry I will taalk to the Javier sir about this aalso. You go and apply leaves."

"I was wondering if I can adjust those compensatory leaves with the other leave!"

"No, no…you go faarward and apply the leaves. Do naat worry about the comp offs."

"Sir, it would be better if you find out and then inform me about the number of compensatory leaves I can get so that I can accordingly plan my trip."

"I taalk to them as soon as paasible. But you go ahead and apply the leaves, aukay," Vishvesh said, still apprehensive about Vimarsh's response.

"Okay sir, I will see what I can do?"

৩৩৩

"Sankat, I waant to know one thing?"

"Yes sir, tell me."

"Can anyone apply for sick leave in one week advance?"

Sankat started laughing, "Sir, this is really a good joke...how can you tell in advance when you are going to get sick?"

Vishvesh laughed meekly, "Yeah, yeah...I was aalso telling my friend the same thing. But he confused me. That izz why I asked you," Vishvesh said. "Sankat, he was asking about some compensation off also. I tells him that when you work on holidays you get those."

༄༅༈

"Madikeri Stop," the conductor announced.

Vimarsh looked at his watch with drowsy eyes. The needle was stuck at half an hour past six in the morning.

The bus station was a small one, with a handful of buses standing at the entrance. Most of the building was either under reconstruction or under construction. Vimarsh didn't care for either. There was an uphill road going from the bus station towards a more formidable plane.

He asked one of the autodrivers about the whereabouts of the freak, who unfortunately was his last hope.

"*Sahib*, very wraang question. You should ask who doesn't know him here," the autodriver replied.

"Okay, what's the tariff?"

"Fix rate for sir's house...twenty bucks. Are you a tourist?"

Vimarsh agreed, not only because he was not in a mood to encourage any more small talk, but also due to the fairly low fare.

The best thing about hill stations is that everything is within walking distance on one main road which acts like the main spinal cord for the town.

The three-wheeler came to a halt after twenty minutes. "Sir, you have to cover some distance on foot along that road," the driver said, pointing at one of the narrow lanes which looked like one of the nerves fanning out from the spinal cord.

The road was like a short pause in a long conversation. On one side of it was a sloping hill originating from the skies with the road appearing as a perfect finale to an absolutely stunning scene; the other side of the road went towards Mother Earth looking like an equally stunning starting point for the visual journey.

A short walk of eight minutes and he was standing in front of a house. The thatched roof was surrounded by plastered walls which were cream in colour. The house was crudely rustic in appearance. On one side of it was a long range of mountains drowned in a blanket of mist. It was simply picturesque; almost unforgettable. Vimarsh thought that even God must have taken a cue from the architectural splendour of heaven when nurturing this place over the years. But then he remembered that God had been far from reasonable, especially in his case.

"Is this Mr Chris Mohan's house?"

"Yes…do you have an appointment?"

"No…not really," Vimarsh stammered.

"Okay, take a seat. Let me inform him."

The small office was decorated with an assortment of coloured candles. Vibrant insignia shimmered aloud from them.

"Hello gentleman," a husky voice echoed in the room, breaking into the thought process of Vimarsh. He turned around to find the owner of the voice standing in front of him. Unlike his usual perception, this real guy was wearing a half-sleeved T-shirt with a large sketch of Che Guevera smiling on it. The pair of khakis were giving an impression of being tortured a lot but still were able to maintain their sheen. The short, spiked hairstyle imparted him a crude yet stylish look and along with a chiselled face, he exuded the confidence that comes from being a success.

"Hello, sir."

"I am Chris Mohan. You can call me Chris," he said, extending his hand.

"Nice to meet you, sir…err…Chris…I am Vimarsh."

"Tell me Vimarsh, why are you here?"

"I had read about you," Vimarsh began, handing over a piece of torn newspaper where the interview was given.

"So you have come here to interview me?"

"Actually you claimed that you can transform anyone into a success in seven days."

"So you have come here to verify my claim," Chris laughed.

"No, actually I was about to give up my life for nothing when I came across this information. So I thought…," Vimarsh stopped abruptly, preferring to keep some details withheld.

"So, either you mean that this interview helped to save your life or you decided to postpone your plan of dying for a few days, after giving me a chance to prove myself."

"No, I mean…I thought I can give it a try," Vimarsh said, trying to sound convincing.

"You think achieving something which seems like a clone of success is some kind of a joke that you can just give a try and back off any moment you don't like the process? Listen carefully, mate, I don't do this stuff for money or glory. I have both in enough measure. When I claimed that I can do it, I put my reputation at stake and I won't let any sucker to spill the water of failure on it because he wants to give it a try before hanging himself from some bloody ceiling."

"I didn't mean that."

"Then what do you mean? Look Vimarsh, I have a seminar to attend and if you can tell me what you really mean, then it will help us both in terms of time and energy."

He kept on looking at Chris with his tongue tied to his lower jaw.

"I am fed up with my life. I don't like myself when I look at the mirror. I hate myself for everything I have done in life. In fact, I have done nothing…NOTHING in life," Vimarsh said, as if waiting to explode any time. "I could not see any way out of this drain. I am weak and tired. If this doesn't change soon, I will have no other option other than…" Vimarsh stopped midway silence. He wanted to say much more but he knew that if he continued further, he might burst into tears.

"How?" Chris was still looking at Vimarsh with a serene expression.

"What how?"

"How would you like to kill yourself? By swallowing pills or poison or by some bullets pumped in your head or do you have any other plan?"

"I don't know...never thought about that," Vimarsh lied, nonetheless amazed at the responses he was getting. He expected either some kind of bashing or preaching in return.

"Okay," Chris said with a thoughtful pause, "we will tell you about that. Don't worry about it right now."

Vimarsh kept on looking at Chris with the same incredulous look in his eyes.

"What do you expect from me? What do you want from me?"

Vimarsh remained quiet for a while. Nobody, in his whole life, had ever asked him WHAT HE WANTED. He choked. Words failed to come out.

"Show me the way to happiness and more happiness. Till now I have known only one way to lead my life and I know it sucks. I know there is another way out but then, there are many locks to which I don't have the keys. I want your help in unlocking them."

"I am still not sure that you can carry the burden of your transformation from your current state to the state you want to achieve."

"I will do whatever you ask me to do."

"My fee is too high."

"I am ready to pay any price."

"It is not money that I seek. Vimarsh, you know what? I will help you, but and this BUT is a big one. How do I know that you are ready to change and won't step back when the going gets tough? There is something else which you need to do before I can rely on your words."

"I will do anything."

"What does your ANYTHING contain?"

"Everything that is possible."

"Can you kill someone?"

A deafening silence engulfed the room.

"If I have to, then I will," Vimarsh spoke after a long pause.

"I am not joking, so think before committing anything within these four walls. I know of people who can kill if one chose to forget one's word…," he paused, maybe for a reply. "If you choose to stay, then my fee is five thousand bucks per day with your signatures on a legal document stating that you will kill the subject. Today you can stay in the guesthouse if you like and can leave tomorrow if you choose. And enjoy Coorg before you leave. It is a very quiet and nice place."

Chris left Vimarsh alone.

21

Day 1

"Nice to see you…*again*. Come on…take a seat. Have some breakfast."

"Chris I want to ask something…," Vimarsh began.

"Later Vimarsh…right now food is priority."

Breakfast was over and the grilling begun.

∽☙∾

"Vimarsh, tell me about your life and any other thing that you may want. But, before that…why did you choose to stay on?"

"Actually, I thought that finally I have nothing to lose."

"Nothing to lose! Interesting."

"I have already been partially dead which made me decide to take my life. Now, when I believe that after going from here, I will have something to cling upon which can change my life, then why not give it my best?"

"So I guess, you are ready to commit."

"Yes, I am."

"You need to sign a document."

Vimarsh nodded.

"…Tell me more about your childhood."

"Err…I don't know where to start?"

"Why not start from the beginning?"

"I was the only child of my parents. They gave me everything. Despite the fact that we were not affluent, I had everything that a child could expect in his perfect childhood. They helped me in making every decision in my life; most of the times, they took the decisions for me. When I was twenty-one, they both died in a car accident. After their death, I felt I had no one left in this world. I became helpless. Nowhere to go. My life went haywire. My relatives tried to help me but I was not comfortable with the idea of accepting them as my surrogate parents."

"Sorry to interrupt you, Vimarsh, but what I have gathered so far is that every decision about your life was taken by your parents and now since they are not here, you find it difficult to take even the smallest step in your life. Please correct me if I am wrong."

"Yes, you are correct."

"By the way, how old are you now?"

"Twenty-seven."

"Okay, go on."

"Then I got this job in a company as a junior accountant. I thought that after some time everything will become alright but things grew worse. My boss, Vishvesh, is an absolute parasite. He has made my life hell. The company has never cared for me. Every month end I get a small paycheck in lieu of my services and sacrifices. My office and my boss are downright exploiters. My colleagues have never cared for me. I know they will be celebrating today as I will not be in office today…"

"So your office never cared for you and they paid you far too less."

"Exactly."

"Your company doesn't pay less but it pays *less to you*."

"What do you mean?"

"In your company, is there anyone who works at the same post as yours but earns three…four or even five times more than you?"

"Yes."

"So what does that imply? It means that your company doesn't pay less; it only pays YOU less."

"I never thought of that." A tingling sensation arose in his body.

"Cursing your life constantly. Even thought of taking your own life. But when YOU yourself are not concerned about your own life or about your own self-esteem, then how do you expect others to respect or acknowledge your existence in their lives?"

Silence.

"And as for your boss...what was his name? Yes, Vishvesh. He is acting like a parasite in your life because you are allowing him to do so...to you and to your life," Chris added. "Vimarsh, answer a simple question. *Do you take hundred per cent responsibility for your life? Whatever has happened to you till now, whatever is happening to you now and whatever will happen to you in future is solely and completely your responsibility and out of your choice, do you agree to it?*" Chris asked, staring at Vimarsh with utmost concentration.

"Yeah...up to some extent," Vimarsh hesitated. He knew that saying 'YES' would snatch away from him his role of a victim and a 'NO' might ruin his chances of staying here.

"The answer is either 'yes' or 'no', not a word more, not a word less," Chris said, staring like a gun at point blank range.

"YES," Vimarsh shouted, sweat shining on his forehead.

"Vimarsh, your life is your responsibility. You have to take action and you have to do whatever it will take to make it memorable. Nobody can do it for you...no one will do it for you...you HAVE to make it happen."

Vimarsh looked into Chris's eyes as if seeing his future reflection in them.

"You have taken the first step in changing your life."

Vimarsh was filled with a renewed vigour.

"What else do you want to be remoulded in your life?"

"There is this girl whom I like, but I don't know how to express it to her?"

"What is her name?"

"I don't know."

"Ever talked to her?"

"Not yet."

"Have you ever talked to any girl?"

"No," Vimarsh remembered the moment when Sheena had scolded him in front of the whole office.

"Okay, then let's see what we have in your menu card for the next fifteen days…Don't look at me with shock. In seven days I can transform you personally but when there is a girl involved, it becomes a totally different ballgame…that's why, fifteen days," Chris said, looking into his black designer diary. "…Since your confidence, self-esteem and desire to live are at an all-time low, so first of all, you need to learn the real recipe for reaching the 'S' word. We will religiously follow a success plan, the self-devised blueprint for everlasting and continuous success **PURPLE-T**© **Technicks**©.

"That will be followed with introduction of **PAP**© **Technicks**© that has the power to change anyone's life with the fairer sex. At the end, I will reveal my self-devised **PCO**© **Technicks**© to take care of your relationships and your personal life. Any queries?"

"Understood."

"There are a few simple rules which you have to follow from now on.

1. Always ask questions.

The one who never asks questions either is unsure about his own intelligence or is smart enough to know everything; though the latter case seldom happens. This also shows that you are interested in the person and want to know more about the subject.

2. If you don't understand something, admit it right away.

If someone talks in Greek, it doesn't mean he is smart. Someone who cannot explain what he wants to tell you in simple words either does not want you to understand it at all or he himself is not clear about it. So better ask. Got it?"

"Yes."

"Moving on, the first **P** stands for a *proactive attitude*. Now what is this proactive thing? Actually it is made up of two words – pro and active. **Pro** means 'forward', according to the dictionary, but to me it means 'someone who is a professional.' **Activity** means 'agility or a state of activeness.' On combining all these, we get a *professionally agile attitude*. So why is this professionally agile attitude the first step towards success? What do you think?"

"All this is a bit heavy for me."

"Okay, let's make it simpler. You know what Abraham Lincoln once said, 'Give me six hours to chop down a tree and I will spend the first four sharpening the axe.' People at the top spend sixty per cent of their time in preparation and forty per cent in taking action. And this kind of attitude is what I call a professionally agile attitude. If you approach each aspect of your life like a professional, success will pursue you, instead of you pursuing it. Keep preparing to position yourself at the right place at the right time – read books, listen to motivational audios, watch motivational videos and inspirational movies. It is not luck, but constant preparation that brings success to one's doorstep. *'Everyone on this planet is unique! Hence no one is smarter than you and no one is better than you.'* And this is your first **chrisanism** of the day."

"**Chrisanism?**"

"A **chrisanism** is something whose truthfulness cannot be contested. It is like a universal fact."

Vimarsh smiled.

"I hope you have understood what the first P contains," Chris concluded.

"Yeah Chris. I had never thought in this manner; I mean this is wonderful. So what is the next Technicks©, I mean 'U'?"

"Not so fast dear. Keep your energy levels high. You will need it when we try to explore the first 'P' in greater depth. But before that, I want you to meet someone who will assist you in your quest for success."

22

"Hi Malvika!"

"Hi Chris! Always bang on time…amazing punctuality. You must be Vimarsh," Malvika said, gleaming with joy.

"Bang on target…like always. Vimarsh, this is Malvika, another asset in your team. She is a bestselling author, perfect wife and mother, a philanthropist and a personality coach. She will help you in everything you need to know about improving your personality and self-confidence. Okay Malvika, I am leaving him in your hands. I have to rush for a meeting. See you later, both of you," and with that Chris left.

"So Vimarsh, before I tell you anything, I want to know what do you think about your dressing, attire and personality?" Malvika began, gesturing him to sit on the nearby chair.

"Malvika*ji*, I have one doubt in my mind……"

"One second Vimarsh*ji*, Malvika is much better."

"Oh sorry, Malvika. I wanted to know why it is important to look good. I mean if you are a good human being, then that is what should matter the most."

"Very good question. Before answering your question, one important thing to remember – use the word '*sorry*' with great care. The thumb rule is '*use the word sorry only five times in a month.*' As for the question you asked, it is one of the many common questions I face from many of my clients in the first meeting. Tell me one thing, will you go and talk to a beggar on your own, when he is covered with mud and filth but has the best heart in the world?"

"Okay, I got your point."

"In eighty per cent of the cases, one never gets the chance to create the much coveted second impression."

"That's why people say first impression is the last impression."

"You can add 'mostly' here. Any other thing that you want to know?"

"Not now. So, from where will we start?"

"We will first work on your dressing style and attire, followed by your walk and other minor things like your handshake. And we need to do something about your weight too. We will hold a session every alternate day till you are confident and knowledgeable about what suits you and what does not."

"That's a great idea…maybe."

"IT IS A GREAT IDEA, I know," Malvika laid emphasis on the first line.

"No, I just remembered something about my boss."

"Okay, so let's start with the basics first."

Malvika then worked with Vimarsh on his weak points, which were many and then after three tiring hours, she asked him to visit her on the third day at the same time.

✎✑✎

"Hi Malvika," Chris was on the telephone that night. He had just returned from the meeting.

"Hi Chris. How was your meeting?"

"It was good, better than expected."

"So do you want to know about Vimarsh's progress?"

"You always sense beforehand what I am thinking. So, how was your session with him?"

"He is really very low on morale. I can't imagine what he must have been like before he met you. He was trying to be positive but, most of the time, negativity and cynicism popped out from him. I could see in his eyes that he was fighting with his beliefs that are now being questioned and tortured by your new theories, just as it happened with me in my initial days, when I was starting all this. Anyhow that was the time when I was trying to find my true purpose in the middle of so much chaos and anarchy in my life."

It was only a few days back when she had been struggling and juggling between her job and her thirteen-month old kid at home and failing in both. She and her husband always felt that they were meant to be something greater in life but with time and increasing responsibilities, all their dreams had gone for a toss. Fortunately, they met Chris and Lekha who helped them to dream again and find ways to realise them. Not only could they fulfil their dreams, but also started dreaming bigger and better.

"I know he is very low on the morale front but I think he will recover, because he is open towards learning. On looking at him, I could clearly see my shadow of my initial days."

"Chris, you have never told me about your struggle," Malvika complained.

"Look at him closely and you will get an idea about how I was ten years back."

"I can't believe that you could be like that."

"I told you earlier also that you wouldn't believe if I was to tell you about my past. Anyway, I am going to take some rest now. Make it a great day tomorrow."

"Bye…you too make it a great day," Malvika said and hung the phone. Her thoughts were now engaged in juggling over Chris's life ten years back. What could have prompted him to change and who was his mentor?

Chris used to tell her that his mentor had expressed his desire to remain anonymous and so could not reveal the name to anyone. But this did not prevent Chris and Lekha to take a month-long holiday to go and meet his mentor in Fiji.

23

Day 2

"Good morning," Vimarsh greeted Chris.

"A very good morning to you too, dude," Chris replied.

"So, when are we going to start with the next Technick©?"

"Relax Vimarsh. At first, I want you to write those things which you have liked about your life till now."

"That's easy. The answer is 'nothing'."

"Try to think of something that you have liked because without that list, we won't go to the next step. The ball is now in your court. Enjoy your breakfast till then," Chris said and sat down to eat his share of the food.

'What do I like about my life?' Vimarsh thought, scratching his head with his pen, sitting in the garden. *'Well, one thing I like is being able to come here and meet Chris and Malvika. What might be the second one?'*

The sun had painted the sky in bright orange when Vimarsh finally got up from his place. That simple question had proved too troublesome for him and almost taken his half day. He felt irritated and infuriated at such wastage of time and so much of money over only fifteen days.

"Hi Lekha! Where is Chris?"

"He has gone to meet one of his friends. Have something till then; he might be arriving soon."

"No, I feel like having a bath. These are the answers to the question Chris had asked me in the morning," Vimarsh said and handed over a sheet to Lekha, irritation visible on his face.

༺✿༻

"Vimarsh has asked me to give you this," Lekha said, handing over the sheet to Chris.

"Good. Looks like he had done a lot of scribbling and deleting on this."

"Do you really think he has in him what you need?"

"Don't know; may be or may be not."

"He was looking a lot irritated when I met him one hour ago."

"Ask him to come in the study room in the next ten minutes."

༺✿༻

"Hi Vimarsh, I was going through your sheet. You have written so many other things but only two that you like in life. And one of them is thinking about her, whose name is still a mystery to you."

"I don't like anything about my life…I told you this the very first day we met."

"Read this…," Chris handed an old piece of paper to Vimarsh, ignoring his emotional outburst.

"What is this?"

"This is what I wrote ten years ago. I was just like you or maybe even worse, with no job, no house, no money and nobody to look up to."

Vimarsh looked at the paper. A numbered list of eighteen things, in tiny letters, was scribbled on it.

"You wrote all this when you had nothing to look forward to in your life? I mean no job, no money and no friends?"

"I was also reluctant just like you but my *guru* made me ponder deeply and extract these eighteen things from my life. And this paper…here…changed my life forever. I came to know that my net worth, which was negative at that time since I was floundering under immense debts and my self-worth were not the same thing. Earlier

I believed both these things to be one and the same thing. I realised then that I had my mind, my health and my spirits with me even if I had no materialistic objects to show off."

"Chris…," Vimarsh took a deep breath to utter the name.

"Take your time Vimarsh, but be loyal to yourself."

"I will try my best."

"The word 'try' is for losers. When you say 'I will try', it means that you are planning never to do it in your lifetime."

"Point noted."

"Let's go for dinner. Lekha must be waiting," Chris said, keeping that precious yellow and torn paper on his shelf as a valuable piece.

Day 3

"Today I am going to tell you only one story. It is a true story about a woman, over seventy-nine years of age and a Catholic nun by profession. She is known as Sister Madonna," Chris began.

Vimarsh smiled.

"She is known to be Iron Nun. It is not because she had taken part in an iron-man competition; she is an iron nun because she had completed more than forty iron-man races," Chris grinned.

"Wait a second…what is this iron-man race?" Vimarsh was obviously hearing the name for the first time.

"Iron-man race? Iron man races entail participating in triathlons which include swimming a length of 2.4 miles and covering 112 miles on a bike followed by a 26 mile-run. All in all, it means more than twenty hours of real agony and pain. And Sister Madonna completed these gruelling races more than forty times. Till forty-seven years of age, she didn't even do any workouts or exercises. Then a priest suggested she should run for attaining spiritual enrichment and gradually she started liking it. At the age of fifty-two, she learned swimming and cycling too. And then within a year she started taking part in triathlons.

"Seventy-two and she was participating in another of these at Hawaii. She almost covered two-thirds of her way in the race, when the wind started picking up. Hawaii, being an island and after witnessing numerous volcanic eruptions in the past, is a very desolate kind of place. The wind soon turned into a monster, blowing at a speed of 56 kms per hour, beating against her frail body. She was only five feet two inches in height and within seconds, she almost became a flying nun. Suddenly a gush of powerful wind literally threw her back and she landed on stones and rocks on the coast, fractured her clavicle, broke her hip joints and cut her face. They took her to the hospital immediately. The following year, to prevent such accidents, the race committee imposed an age limit of sixty-years for participating in the competition. So when she went for the race next year, they didn't allow her to sign up, so she decided to race along with the other participants without a badge number and completed the entire race. Just because of her determination, the committee had to revoke the age-limit rule."

There was a deafening silence in the room as Chris paused for breath. "Just think of it for a moment – through her sheer willpower and courage she made the whole committee to rescind on their decision and even change it back," Chris said, again pausing for a minute to let the idea sink in.

"Is it true?" Vimarsh asked, looking bewildered.

"Believe in your instincts, on whatever they tell you."

"But how could she undertake this herculean task at her age?"

"That is the secret hidden of 'U', which we will unearth today."

"You mean her indomitable spirit was the result of 'U' captured in the PURPLE-T© Technicks©?"

"Vimarsh, no success can't be without this 'U'. All the thriving successes are only a byproduct of it."

"What is that secret? Tell me…I am dying to know it."

"U in PURPLE-T© Technicks© stands for **Undertaking Inspired Action**. A fair idea with action undertaken to complete it is far better than a brilliant idea with no action supporting it."

"But Chris, this is something that everyone knows about, so how can it be a secret?"

"I know every person has heard of this in his or her lifetime but still, how many follow it? How many of us stop daydreaming and start taking action? My guess is…only a handful," Chris said, looking at Vimarsh, who was in his usual thinking mode.

"It is true. Even in my case, I always knew where I was lacking but still when I contemplated committing suicide, that I was woken up. So that's why it is a secret. But what is meant by *inspired* action?" Vimarsh said thoughtfully.

"Absolutely Vimarsh, that is why it is a secret. It's out in the open for all but still we are unaware of it. By coming here you have started the action process but your efforts would go in vain if you were not to practice these secrets. So it is a continuous process for whose success you have to continue taking action. It is like brushing your teeth daily because one day of sloppiness will leave your mouth stinking. It is inspired because you are doing something that you have been inspired to do. When you love what you do, it makes that whole process a cakewalk."

Vimarsh seemed unsure about the inspired aspect.

The following small incident might help to understand it further.

A new person joined as a salesman in a company in the introductory phase of the company. The trainer encouraged everyone to toss as many doubts as they could. The weak-looking kid hoped that someone would ask his question also in that rain of doubts.

Alas! No one asked.

The session was about to end when he raised his hand with utmost sincerity on his face.

"Shoot your query, kid," the instructor encouraged him.

"How can one sell a product if one doesn't like the product oneself?"

The instructor gave him a saintly smile. The kid looked confused and scared as all eyes were fixed on him in a what-is-this-crap look. The instructor drew close to him and patted his shoulder softly before replying, "You can't," Chris concluded.

"But how does one prepare oneself for taking inspired action? Isn't it too much of a task to move our lazy bones?" Vimarsh asked.

"So many ifs and buts. Okay Vimarsh, have you ever thought about something you were not happy with and felt that the more you thought about it, the more it made things worse?"

"Yes, all the time."

"That's because when you have one sustained thought, Nature immediately brings more *like* thoughts to you. In a matter of seconds, you are surrounded with more unhappy thoughts and the situation seems to worsen. The more you think about it, the more you get upset. You also might have experienced attracting *like* thoughts when watching some movie, and then finding that you couldn't get over some scene in that movie. It keeps playing on and on. That is because when you were watching that scene, without realising it, your full attention was focused on it. While doing so, you attracted more *like* thoughts about that scene. So bring more thoughts in your mind that will help you attract more and more action-oriented thoughts and eventually you will have no choice but to take action because *we become what we think.*"

"So, I need to get more empowering thoughts in my head."

"Now you are getting it right."

"I guess so, but I still have a long way to go."

"The time to complete this journey is directly proportional to the efforts you put in."

❧

Day 4

"What is insanity?"

"I don't know exactly, but I think it is related to madness."

"It is doing the same thing again and again while expecting a different result every single time. Each one of us follows the same approach in making decisions every time. We expect profits from our previous bad decisions. We commit the same mistake in our relationship, expecting it to survive, come what may. Vimarsh, when you will undertake action with a professionally agile attitude, you will find yourself in a soup full of errors and failures. You might fall down hundreds of times before tasting even a tiny speck of success. Sometimes even the simplest of your thoughts will seem far-fetched and difficult to follow, but you must look at the bigger picture. At those trying times, your ultimate goal will give you the courage to move ahead and not stop. You have to work continuously on realising and rectifying your errors while building your dreams with new passion and energy. That is the meaning of the word 'R' in **Recognising and Rectifying Mistakes.**"

"How can I succeed in rectifying my errors after I have figured them out?"

"There is a simple four-step process for you to follow while you are in the process of handling the failure.

- Recognise where you have gone wrong.
- Figure out the factors that lead to failure (it also includes the emotions).
- Chalk out a strategy to fill in the gaps.
- Find a new way of doing things if your old way fails to provide an effective result. In other words, don't be *insane*."

"What about the disappointments which will arise due to constant failures? How can one motivate oneself when encountering such numerous road blocks?" Vimarsh asked, thinking of his past life which only consisted of let downs…twenty-seven difficult years of continuous disappointments and agony.

"I was expecting this, but don't worry. We will cover this also but not today. The next two days will be devoted to your question," Chris assured.

~◦◦~

Day 5

"Till now we have covered 'P', 'R', 'U' of *PURPLE-T*© during the last four days. The building blocks of the base are now complete and we are ready to move on towards starting the building now," Chris said as he wrote the three letters on the board.

"Chris, I have one question."

"Yes, Vimarsh?"

"I read somewhere that one should make use of the other person's name as often as possible while talking to him. Any special reason for that?"

"Vimarsh, the best thing to give any person is to respect his individuality. By using his name, you accept his presence and earn respect in return. My dear friend, *you get what you give*. Simple law of giving and receiving."

Vimarsh had now entered the stage of introspection. Vishvesh could never remember anyone's name and this was one of the main reasons why he was most despised in the whole office.

"Okay, now we can move on to the next 'P'," Vimarsh said.

Chris smiled and said, "Yesterday, you asked me how to motivate a person who is encountering numerous road blocks. The secret lies in the second 'P' of **PURPLE-T**©. It stands for **persistence**. Persistence is THE MASTER KEY for opening any lock," Chris said and wrote it in block letters on the board.

"Why is the master key in caps?"

"Since this is the single point differentiating the poor from the rich, a millionaire from a billionaire and a failure from a success."

"But how is persistence responsible for this?"

"The dictionary tells us 'persist' means 'to continue firmly or obstinately in an opinion or a course of action in spite of difficulty, opposition, or failure.' If one is adamant about achieving something in his life, he or she, irrespective of the gender, will get what he or she wants. The successful persons I am referring to had faced their share of failures. Some failures were so big and catastrophic that they were reduced to rags from riches or even worse. I suspect those on the other side of the fence may not have such failures and even if they did, it was the last time they took any risk because subsequently they lived their life safely ensconced, taking no risks AT ALL. You were a failure. I am not saying this to embarrass you, but you have been the worst failure

I have ever seen in my life and that includes the man in the mirror. The reason is simple. You never made any effort to change your situation. You wasted all these years without any substantial effort to work hard. Had you persisted in any of the areas long enough or had you taken even one step a week, you never would have needed me. You would have saved your money, you time and the guilt of an imminent murder."

Vimarsh winced at the last word, nevertheless keeping his gaze on Chris.

"Persistence is the key; it is the MASTER KEY and the only KEY between success and failure. You will fail, even if I were to teach you every single trick from my bag, if you don't persist after going from here. Trust me and rely on me blindly when I say this. I can tell you numerous stories about how persistence changed people's lives but I won't do so now since stories are in the past. You are your present. Your present is a present to you by this universe and the sooner you start treating it like one, the better your future would become."

Vimarsh sat dumbstruck, absolutely dumbstruck. He had enough to ponder over the weekend when Chris would have left on his travels to various cities for attending seminars.

He had to write his goals for his last few days in this world – a task entrusted to him for the weekend.

Strangely enough, a week had already passed.

Day 6

Vimarsh had just got over his busiest weekend in his twenty-seven summers. "Hello Vimarsh, how are you?"

Vimarsh had not seen Chris since the past two days. Obviously he had been travelling and Vimarsh had no idea when he would be back.

"I have not been able to sleep since the last two days. This was the busiest weekend of my life till now. And do you know, what was the best thing? I never felt so energised and focused in my life till now."

"Average people consider work on weekdays as enough to take care of their lives. But success asks you to work 24x7, not physically though. Weekends are your gateway to success. You work for your company, for your bank, for your luxuries on weekdays and *work for yourself, on yourself and by yourself on weekends.*"

"But I am confused as to why you asked me to write my goals in present tense, as if I had achieved them all?"

"The answers lies in the 'L' of **PURPLE-T**©."

"What is that?"

"The 'L' stands for '**Law of Expectancy**'."

"Law?"

"Have you ever experienced that when you don't want to see someone, he still keeps on appearing from somewhere again and again? Have you ever felt that the thing you dread the most happens always at the wrong time and keeps on happening persistently to you?"

"The thing I dread the most is reaching office late and facing Vishvesh. So since the morning, I keep saying to myself, 'I don't want to be late. I don't want to be late' but something or the other keeps on happening. No matter how early I leave home, I invariably reach office late or my boss reaches before me."

"Not only to you, such things happen to all of us. The thought uppermost in our mind keeps on happening at the right or wrong time in our lives. This is the Law of Expectancy and whether you know it or not, believe it or not, or even if you decide to ignore it, this law is always working in our lives. *If you persistently bring some particular thought in your mind, you will keep getting it in your real life too.*

"Our human mind is like a magnet which attracts every feasible event towards itself and whose frequency is matched with the frequency of our thoughts. Our mind manifests our every thought, no matter whether it is good or bad since our mind does not process the 'NOT' word while manifesting our thought. It is like that law of gravity. If someone falls from a twenty-storey building, it doesn't matter whether he is good or bad. He will hit the ground anyways. The law works even when you don't want it to work.

"Similarly LOVE is very precise and always present. If you love to think how much deprived you are or how much impoverished you are, you will remain so."

"Chris, does that mean that whatever happens in our lives is only because of the thoughts we attract in our lives?"

"Absolutely."

"But then why is it that so many people die at the same time?"

"In any calamity many people lose their lives. It happens because many of them must have had such thoughts in their minds and the frequency of their thoughts coincided with the frequency of that event. Quantum physics tells us that the entire universe emerged from thought. So it is not any good or bad luck. I always tell all my clients to *watch their thoughts* more than they watch their words."

"But we think all the time. Isn't it impossible to check all our thoughts?"

"Absolutely and you might be amazed to know that a normal human being thinks about 60,000 thoughts a day. We can check our thoughts if we concentrate on our feelings. If we are happy, it is impossible to fill our mind with destructive thoughts in life or vice versa. So always ask yourself, 'How am I feeling?' If the answer is, 'I am feeling good,' then keep on doing it. Also, always think about what you want in life, not about what you don't want. Thoughts about what you want will manifest your wants for you."

"So you mean that my goals will be manifested on the dates I choose them to be?"

"Even better. In seventy per cent of the cases, these will come true before the stipulated date. Even Albert Einstein and Sir Isaac Newton believed in this law. Einstein once said, *Reality is merely an illusion, albeit a very persistent one.*"

"So I can get anything I want, if I want it desperately enough? Is that what you mean?"

"Yes, that's exactly what I mean."

"You mean *anything*?"

"ANYTHING. PERIOD."

Vimarsh's mind did a double take. ANYTHING? He could ask for anything and it would manifest.

Then why can't I live for 90 years? Why do I have to die within three months or so?

🙣🙠

Day 7

"The 'E' stands for '**Endless Preparation**'. But why endless?" Chris asked, beginning the day's proceedings. "Death and opportunity always come unannounced. This is as true as the fact the sun rises from the east. I have seen cases where one of the biggest opportunities knocked on one's door but the person was afraid to open the door and unprepared to take advantage of it. I have seen people with the next best idea about a new technology, about a book or some other product but unable to take action when the opportunity came knocking on their door. They chose to go into oblivion forever rather than opening the door and letting the opportunity in. History tells us of actors, writers, entrepreneurs who were talented and capable to make a mark in this world but not prepared enough to justify their talents in the large arena of life. I have also seen people preparing all through their lives and waiting for their big break. Successful actors, writers, entrepreneurs and painters keep on persisting and honing their skills till the right time comes to strike and then they shine like crazy diamonds."

Vimarsh was still not convinced.

"Don't trust me blindly. Pick up the day's newspaper and you will find that for every Sachin Tendulkar, there are numerous clones of him – some even better than him when he was of their age. But then, he practices and prepares himself daily over all these years, even after gaining the much-coveted success in the annals of sports. Others just fizzled out when the time came to show their mettle. The preparation phase comes before the opportunity phase. In reality, you don't pursue success. No, not at all. Pursuance of success is futile and wastage of time. You can only attract success by becoming an attractive person."

"Attracting the success? That is news for me."

"Truth is always like news. So how can you become an attractive person? The answer is simple. By preparing endlessly to embrace the truth and the subsequent breaks. Do something every day towards self-improvement, no matter how tiny the difference it makes. In baseball, a study showed that the best players earned almost ten times than an average player. Also some other statistics revealed that out of every twelve strikes, an average player touches the ball three times; only three times out of twelve, while the best in the business hits the ball four times – only four times out of the same twelve. The difference of a single hit creates a difference of almost ten times in their earnings and hence in their lifestyle."

Vimarsh finally gave an understanding smile.

"That is the power of small progress – a tenfold increase in the end results," Chris concluded. "Today is the day when I complete explaining the PURPLE-T© and you will start exploring it."

"But Chris, there is one last 'T' still left."

"I was about to come to it and since you are already using it from the day you came here, I think you can explain it to me."

Vimarsh looked confused.

"Try to think harder that what this T could probably mean?"

"Team!" Vimarsh said unsurely.

"Well, in every way, you are right…T stands for '**Team**'. Yes, a seemingly innocent word – team. Since childhood we have been programmed to abhor teamwork. In exams it is also known as cheating. Our school system is designed to de-motivate teamwork. That's why many-high performers eventually turn out to be job worshippers while many college dropouts become millionaires. A job is primarily a single-person activity. Even if you are not comfortable with your teammates, you can still survive in your job. In business, if you don't collaborate with other people's expertise, you will be responsible for the failure of your venture as you cannot run it all alone. People who try to do everything on their own in a business finally end up owning their single shop and confining themselves into a dull and monotonous routine from morning to night. A true leader collaborates with the people who are best in their fields. He knows that he can't do everything, like accounting or finance or HR or administration entirely on his own."

"But how am I related to this analogy?" Vimarsh asked, still confused.

"In your case, your team consists of Malvika and me. You already know what the end result was when you were operating alone. Each one of us believes that no one can do it with greater perfection than he can but the reality is that even if we know everything and can do it alone, it is best to delegate certain tasks to the specialists and trust them that they will do it in the best possible way. Yes, choosing them is one of the key requisites of an able brain and a totally different area to cover, maybe some other time," Chris concluded.

"So, you have planned well enough to entice me to come here again soon," Vimarsh laughed.

"Once a salesman, always a salesman."

∾☙∾

Day 8

"Vimarsh, today I am going to tell you a new secret about the fair sex."

"A secret about how to treat girls?"

"To tell you the most important rule of this game – the game which is going on between us and them, between you and her – and since it is high time to familiarise you with it, we need to go back to the era of human evolution. But first thing first. *It is a setup.*"

"SETUP! What kind of setup?"

"A setup by Nature or our Creator or by someone from our society. I am not sure about the source but definitely it is a setup. Have you ever watched the Discovery Channel?"

"Yes, many times."

"There is one very peculiar aspect. Not only in human beings but in every species, there lies an unspoken bond that before accepting a proposal, the female has the upper hand in the relationship (and in many cases, even after accepting it). The males either have to fight with each other or do something unique to attract her and most of the times there are numerous contenders for the same subject. It is like thirty seconds of glory or gory."

"You mean that this trait is same in humans and animals?"

"Humans are social animals, aren't they?"

"Yes, they are, but…"

"Again but? Okay, all these things do happen in our society but in a slightly subtle manner. The stakes are higher here because if the girl knows about the immense power she holds in her tender hands, then she has the choice of being unapproachable among her peers. You can also call her the alpha female. An alpha female can only be tamed by an alpha male. But till she finds one, she may choose to play with other toys. Now, if she is an alpha, you have only two choices – either to drop out of this game or play to win."

Vimarsh nodded his head vigorously.

"So for an alpha female, you need some special abilities, some special skills that will position you uniquely in front of her. *Remember, the best position is one where you have the option to choose and not be someone else's choice.*"

"Now I know why I am stuck in my job because I am not the chooser. I am the one who gets chosen by someone else and that's why I am so helpless and unhappy about my job and myself."

"Exactly, and now you know in which place you want to see yourself from now on."

"No one has ever made this difference so clear to me."

"That is not anybody's mistake. Ninety-five per cent of us don't know about this and the five per cent who do know this, never divulge this secret due to the fear of losing control over the rest."

"Tell me what I must do to change my place?"

"Well you have already taken the right step towards that end and in the next six days you will learn the **Power Accelerate Principles**© **Technicks**© or **PAP**© **Technicks**© that teach how to master this art," Chris said, pausing for a minute. "First rule – *NEVER CRITICISE.*"

"Even if it is constructive criticism?"

"Even if it is constructive. You are not her father or uncle or brother or some friend and you don't want to be one either."

"But why not as a friend? What's wrong in being a friend?"

"People say, love is friendship. I say, for ordinary girls it maybe true but for an alpha, once you become a friend, you become a non-existent glitch in her happening life."

"Understood…NO GLITCH."

"Her slip-ups are only her way of manipulating things according to her desires and fancies. She loves to tease you. If you fall for that, then she will take charge; not you. She might let you feel that you are in control, but behind the veil of her innocent smile she holds the remote control. If you criticise her, it would simply encourage her to play with you."

"But how? If I am the person who is asking her to mend her ways, then I am the person who is in charge. Right?"

"Right but wrong; absolutely off the target. Let's take a hypothetical situation where she does something which you have forbidden her to do. How will you react?"

"I will ask her to stop doing it."

"And she will give you her cutest smile and continue doing it. What would you do then?"

"I will ask her sternly to stop it."

"Again the same reaction from her would come, followed by a small peck on your cheek. Now what?"

"I might smile and let her do her thing."

"And lose control over the situation. Right? If you had done nothing in the first place and skipped to the last step directly, you would have achieved the same thing and also kept the control to yourself."

"But that is insane. If I were not to tell her that what she is doing is wrong, then who will?"

"That is a good question. If you do not, then who will? The answer is that it is not your headache. Look Vimarsh, *the one who has the stick has everything*. If you don't have the stick, then somebody else will."

"And the one who has the stick has the power," Vimarsh added.

"So if you want the stick, then you have to work smartly. The first five minutes of your conversation decide who will take charge of the stick. After those five minutes, one of you will lead and the other will follow just as you see in a couple's dance."

"Only five minutes!"

"Five minutes is the average time limit, though it may vary from ninety seconds to seven minutes. Our aim is to gain the upper hand in less than ninety seconds."

"I am still coping with the five-minute deadline and you are saying that I should aim for a minute-and-a-half. You are really impossible."

"I am not impossible. I am a realist who knows what is possible and what is not. So let's start."

"As you say…*sir,*" Vimarsh said sarcastically.

"Okay Vimarsh, since Malvika has already guided you towards a right presentation, we must team it up with a right persona and correct attitude."

For Vimarsh, every passing minute was opening a world of new possibilities in front of his eyes.

The discussion ended only when Lekha called them for dinner for the fifteenth time.

ॐ

Day 9

"Good morning, Chris."

"Good morning Vimarsh."

"How are you?"

"A little heady about what you said yesterday, but equally excited to know the next step."

Chris smiled.

"The next secret is simple…*BE YOURSELF*. Once you realise the power of being in control, this one principle will take you to that place swiftly. It will also keep you grounded. You will start enjoying everlasting success while focusing on reaching still greater heights."

"Be yourself," Vimarsh repeated. "But Chris, this is quite a simple rule. How can it be a secret then?"

"Yes, it is a very common phrase among common people but how many people follow these two words? Most of us tend to agree with the bullshit that is thrown at us by our boss or colleagues or anyone else and rather than confronting it or presenting our viewpoints and being ourselves, we blindly accept it. It is a herd mentality. We all want someone else to lead us. That is why we love Spiderman and Super-man, because we expect our leaders to be like them – all white and no black. However, in this chaos, we tend to forget that our leaders are also humans endowed with their share of good qualities co-existing with bad qualities. As a matter of fact, they are grey from inside rather than being just black or white. If you look at Nature, to maintain the balance, there is a Raavan for every Rama and a Kansa for every Krishna. They are the symbols to show that darkness and light coex-ist in universe. We are living in a leader-hungry nation, but we forget that each one of us has the ability to be a leader; in other words, be a superman. Instead of aping someone else, I am asking you to be true to yourself and soon you will find others following you. That is why it is very important to understand the meaning of these two words."

"All my life, I wanted somebody to guide me, to hold my hand and help me confront all adversities. But today, when I think over it, I feel how foolish and stupid I was and still am," Vimarsh said, walking down memory lane.

"Vimarsh, I can understand your position. I too have been through these things once. So, if you are shy, remain shy; if you are an introvert, remain one. Just BE YOURSELF. If she has acknowledged your presence in her life, then she has already accepted you for what you are. Now, your only objective is not to make an impression but rather not to mess it up."

Day 10

"The third rule is not only applicable in the case of girls, but is also very important in your personal and professional life – *ALWAYS GO FIRST CLASS*. Your team has already worked on you to make you first class. Now it is your attitude which should be in sync with your new look.

"Always remember these three tenets:

- Always dress for the place you want to see yourself in the near future; never for the place in which you are right now.
- You are neither right nor wrong because people agree or disagree with you.
- No one is smarter than you and no one is better than you."

Chris took a short pause to let it settle down. "Okay, let's break it into meaningful chunks. Vimarsh, when you came here and now when you see yourself after ten days, do you decipher any change in your looks or your personality?"

"Lots of."

"Tell me about it."

"Well, Malvika has helped me a lot in changing my attitude towards my physical appearance. She has taught me to choose the right attire. I mean, how to look casual and yet be in control. Because of her, I have learned about the things which were obstructing my efforts to fructify. I have also realised that cleanliness goes a long way in one's life. Clean teeth, fresh breath, no body odour, correct weight and a well-maintained look are the key to success.

"Women notice all these details. For men, there is only one 'blue' but for women there is a sky blue, dark blue, indigo blue, peacock blue, navy blue, light blue. They notice everything – even minor things like whether your belt and shoe match or not. Your body odour, eating style, likes and dislikes, that is, every damn thing is marked, remembered and their final decision is based on the minutest of these details. Whether you like it or not, they simply don't operate in any other way. So nail these before you even think of approaching them. *Always go first class.*"

࿄

Day 11

"IT IS ONLY A NUMBER GAME. As a salesman, initially I faced continuous rejections. You must have noticed people entering the showroom to buy a car but returning without buying one. So I felt like a car, which has been rejected every day despite putting in so much of hard work. One day my manager called me and said, *'Chris, this is only a stupid game. You only have to count the number of rejections before you get one that will eventually say YES. You get 25 per cent of the gross profit on the deal. That means if the total profit is 50k, then your commission is 12,500. If you have been rejected nine times before getting that much-awaited YES, then think of it in this way that you are getting 12,500 by 10 equalling 1,250 for every NO.'*

"This simple mathematics changed my whole perspective towards rejection. I started looking forward to every rejection since I realised that I was getting paid for it. If at any time you contemplate approaching a girl in a public place and all kinds of negative thoughts enter your head, like being rejected by her or her jealous boyfriend kicking your ass or she treating you as a loser or giggling among her friends while ignoring you completely, just remember that it is only a number game, Out of the 1,000 women you meet, there will be some women who are not interested in relationships; some will be married or engaged; some may be lesbians; some are cold; some are angry with past relationships and some are plainly not interested in anything new. In the remaining 30 per cent, only 15 per cent will be friendly and nice to you. So, just move on if you face a 'NO'. Hell will not break lose if someone rejects you and you will not be doing anything which no one has done before. Even an average-looking woman can be a subject of fantasy of many, so it is nothing new for them. They like being flirted with, pampered or attended. They will be pretty cool with the idea of some guy falling for them. Got it?"

"Completely."

Day 12

"Human nature is such that it gets attracted to things which are mysterious. Rekha, the yesteryear actress, is one living example and so is Marlyn Monroe and Elvis Presley. Their secret lifestyle and their unusual life made them living legends. Once we know everything about someone, we lose interest. Once we know what will be their next reaction or can deduce the next sentence from their mouth, there is no novelty."

"Then how do you achieve it?"

"That depends...'

"*On me*...I know," Vimarsh interrupted.

"Exactly. You have to invent and reinvent *yourself* every day. Think outside the box, inside the box or turn the box upside down but think of ideas to keep you alive and others astounded. The key is to **be different** in an attractive way."

"My question is how to do it?" Vimarsh was still adamant.

"Okay, let's start with what not to do. One thing you can do to sabotage your prospects is to crave for her attention. If you go somewhere along with her where she knows everyone and you don't, like a party or an art exhibition where she is the expert and you are just a companion to her, give her plenty of space. Don't follow her everywhere like a satellite. If she starts talking to someone, move on to the bar or stay back, while keeping an eye on her. You don't want to be caught fooling around when she searches for you to introduce you to someone in the party. So maintain the eye contact from a distance and enjoy yourself. You will seem like a confident guy with high self-esteem, but don't get engrossed in some random discussion that makes you forget that you are not alone in the party. Talk to people but remember your main aim is to be with her. After the party or show, don't rush for a taxi or something. Walk a little, seek her opinion on what she liked, what she felt. And when she tells you, do not look at her lips or think how lucky you are to be with her; focus on what she is saying so that you can respond when it's your turn. Listening to her is the key. Women love to talk about things you consider unimportant. So listen what they speak and respond. *Listen and respond.*"

"Listen and respond," Vimarsh repeated.

"Put forth your opinion without worrying about displeasing her, but don't drag it for long. Women like men who are in control. Show her that you have your own mind. It's okay to be frank but at the same time, don't overdo it. It might hurt you."

"So it is all about mixing everything right."

"Exactly and this might not be a discovery for anyone sensible but pretty girls are asked out all the time. They are the spoilt breed. They are so used to getting pampered that something like spanking them whenever they misbehave can create magic. Remember this is your space and she is just a visitor. Here you lay down the rules; not her."

Day 13

"Final step before a new beginning: *'claim your place'* in her world. There is nothing like a *'just friend'*. 'Just friends' means that you both are in a pseudo dating mode which is a pre-stage before going into either the dating mode or back to the *'hopeless friends'* mode. It is your duty to lead the game by telling her that your relationship is at 'just friends' stage, since it is important that who says it first, as he/she then has the power to call the shots. It is important to gear up or gear down according to the circumstances. When it gets too hot to handle, diffuse the situation by dropping the bomb of *'just friends'* and when it is too cold, take the pressure away by mixing flirtation and friendship. Give her subtle hints that you like her but she is not the only one for you. Play along this theme till she begs you to stop it. Also, don't make her the centre of your daily life but try to be the centre for her in all the activities. It is important that you should be seeing at least three to four girls at the same time."

Vimarsh laughed sarcastically.

"Right now I am struggling to see even a single aunty type in my life and you want me to flirt with three or four girls at one time?"

"If she knows that she is your focus, then you don't need a devil in your life. Even if you carry the relationship forward, you will always be at her command. So allow the confusion to prevail in her mind as it will pave the way for your victory. And don't worry about the other girls. It is always better to have more options at your disposal."

"But does it not amount to two-timing or double date?"

"Dude, first thing is you are in a pre-dating mode or the 'just friend' mode. Secondly, it is just a game which is not created by you or me. Only the fittest survives in this game. If you are not fit, be ready to make room for someone better."

Vimarsh looked unconvinced but Chris still moved on.

"Women categorise men as
- Uninterested.
- A good friend.
- A husband.
- A boyfriend."

"What's the difference between third point and fourth?"

"Let me ask you something: where do you see yourself with respect to her?"

"I want to marry her, obviously."

"You know what the interesting part is? If a woman sees you as husband material, she will usually hold back the sex but if she considers you as boyfriend material, she will be open to sexual relations soon enough and is likely to enter into a long-term relationship with you. In case you approach her for third point, then you will take her to dinner, buy her gifts, will get romantic and other things. And you will kill your chances since everyone else is also doing the same. Why should she be attracted to you? What is different about you that others are not giving her? I mean, think why some soap is better than the others when they all do the same thing? Still you buy one brand and not the other. Selling and marketing. There the soap is the product and here the product is YOU."

"You mean everything is selling."

"Every single damn thing. You sell yourself to get a job, to get accepted in society, to win friends, to get bank loans, to get promotions and virtually every other thing."

"So the fourth point is the key."

"No," Chris snapped.

"NO!"

"The key is YOU. Everything else is only a way to reach her."

"But isn't it bad to manipulate her?"

"Did she ever look at you till now…EVER?"

"NO."

"And till now you have not played any games with her?" Chris asked but Vimarsh remained silent.

"I told you, this setup is not created by me."

"I got it."

"These are the six rules. This is a science which, if you follow, will make you succeed but this is also an art since this is not the only way to success. You can always find your own paths or modify the existing ones."

༄༅࿆

Day 14

"Two more days are left for your training to complete. You have almost completed it and rather successfully. Today we are going to explore a method to create a long-lasting and effective relationship. It is called as **PCO© Technicks©**. P for Pamper. C for Care. O for Own."

"Pamper, Care, Own," Vimarsh repeated.

"First step: pamper the person you care for with love, respect and dignity. Give him or her what he or she wants but do not do it under pressure or any fear that if you do not appease her, she will leave you for better prospects. That does not happen in a relationship else it would tantamount to blackmailing. So better let go of such people from your life."

Vimarsh remembered Nick.

"Care for them in the most genuine way, without trying to change them or changing yourself for them. Be yourself and let them be themselves. That is the second part. Accept them for what they are. That is the real sense of caring."

Vimarsh's mind wandered off to his past but not for long.

"And finally win them, win their faith, their honesty and their love for you. It is far better than controlling your or their emotions for your petty ego. This last step will happen automatically if you take care of the first two."

Vimarsh had no words to express his gratitude to Chris.

~☙~

Day 15

"Congratulations, today is the last day of your training."

"It was the best journey of my life."

"Vimarsh, today I am not going to lecture you on anything but I want you to take up a challenge, which will test you and assure me that my method still works if put into action – '*90 days challenge©*'. Today is 2nd October and you have with you exactly ninety days to fulfil this challenge, which will be by the time this year ends. The objective is to create a mini life – a life within a life of ninety days which knows only one thing and that is '*Excellence Explosion©*'. This stage of your life is the pivot from which you can only ascend to greater heights and reap unimaginable fruits. This universe started from a single explosion, the 'Big Bang' and so will be your journey. Think of an unimaginable goal to reach in the coming ninety days. The magnanimity of that goal will take you out of your comfort zone and trust me, you will achieve it if you dedicate yourself completely to it. Just follow the principles I have told you."

Vimarsh sat, listening intently.

"One question bothers me a lot – if you are on your deathbed, what would you remember? Obviously you won't remember the number of hours you spent in office or in singing phony praises of your boss or playing dirty office politics to advance in job. But you will definitely remember your friends' faces and the lives you touched and improved; the stars you counted on a dark night, sitting next to the love of your life; the fights and arguments with your parents over a bicycle or a mobile phone; the people you loved and got loved. But, by then it will be too late to do anything about it even if you were not satisfied with the answers. Learning from these points, I resolved to do it all much earlier in life and not once, but every month, twelve times a year. I ask myself every day, 'What have I done last month? Did I touch anyone's life for good? Did I achieve something worthwhile? Did I give enough love and such questions?' And I ask you to do the same from now on."

Vimarsh's eyes turned moist. He had only three months to live and he had learned the important aspects of life in just these three weeks.

'*What will I remember?*' he wondered!

❦

"Good morning, Vimarsh."

"A very good morning to you too."

"So, from today you are going to be responsible for your successes and failures."

"I can't tell you how keyed up I feel."

"I am happy that you have identified the real you in these three weeks."

"A shift in attitude is only possible by a similar shift in your attitude."

"A display of nice and clear thinking once again. Anyway, tomorrow I have some work in Bangalore, so I plan to accompany you."

"Meanwhile I was thinking of meeting Malvika."

"Sure, I will catch you in the evening. One more guy is there waiting for me; may be he faces the same dilemmas."

"I sincerely hope you will help him in choosing the right tools for committing suicide."

"I guess so," Chris said, with a poker face.

❦

"What have you thought about dinner?" Chris asked Vimarsh. They were about to touch their base at Bangalore.

"There is one Pizza Hut near my place."

"That will be good; it's been a long time since I have had any," Chris chuckled.

"Vimarsh, here is the package with all the details about your target," Chris said after they got over.

Vimarsh looked horrifically at the brown envelope, about which he had almost forgotten. Maybe, he thought, it was just another way of Chris to scare him away. He quietly kept it in his bag.

"All the best for your new life," Chris said.

Vimarsh smiled meekly.

24

It was already midnight but Vimarsh was wide awake.

"Why the hell are you still awake?" Nick asked on entering the room.

"I don't want to talk at the moment."

"Even I don't want to argue at night, but I am not sure whether you still want to die or not."

"I said I don't want to talk," Vimarsh repeated.

"Okay, fine but in case…"

"GET OUT," Vimarsh screamed.

Nick stumbled on his way out. Vimarsh closed the door. He looked at the brown envelope which he had not opened yet. He tried to sleep but failed miserably again.

The clock struck seven and the alarm clock found itself turned on. Vimarsh woke up, startled. The brown package still lay on his side-table. He looked at it helplessly.

༄෴༅

The clock struck ten and Vimarsh was still in bed.

Finally he tore open the package. A photo and a letter fell out of it.

Vimarsh looked at them as if they were ticking time-bombs. He thought of running out of the room. He felt he was better as a loser because then he was only killing himself. Finally he jumped out of the bed and stared at the face in the photo.

It was of an old man sitting on a Harley Davidson in the biker's gear and looking at him with pleading eyes. The letter contained the address. It was near him now.

༄෴༅

It was almost evening and he decided to finish the task. It was a promise he could not turn down. He felt strange that the three months were now looking so enticing to him.

'This man has already lived his life, so it is better if he dies. I am only twenty-seven; I deserve to live,' he thought.

༄෴༅

He knocked on the door and it opened with a loud creaking noise. A cat jumped out from the tiny opening when the door opened ajar.

"Come inside, Lizzie," a man shouted from inside. The door opened and showed the owner of the voice. He looked younger than the photograph Vimarsh had.

"We don't need anything."

"I am not a salesman, uncle."

"Uncle! Who's uncle? Are you blind?"

"Sorry, sir."

"Okay, okay, come inside. I have some work for you."

Vimarsh looked confused. "*Arrey,* don't be afraid. Come right inside."

Vimarsh had no other option but to obey.

"Rub this balm over my back."

Vimarsh expected a courteous question mark at the end but found a full stop instead. The man lay down on his bed, exposing his wrinkled body.

"What are you looking at?" he snapped, "Hurry up, do it fast."

Vimarsh looked at the pillow lying nearby and remembered the scene from a Hindi movie where Amrish Puri had used the simple weapon to silence his weak detractor.

Vimarsh Puri? Sounded vicious.

"Ahhh…your hands are so soft," the old man moaned with pleasure. "Where do you live?"

"Nearby."

"Come every day at this time. Your hands feel so good…ahhhhh."

Vimarsh glanced away, feeling like a hooker. He cursed Chris wholeheartedly.

"Now you can go and close the door behind you. It is time for me to sleep. My daughter will soon be coming," he said and closed his eyes.

Vimarsh knew that this was his only chance.

෴

"Who are you?" a question startled Vimarsh as he was about to close the door behind him.

He turned abruptly and saw the most beautiful face in his whole life.

"Nothing," he stammered.

"Tell me or I will call the police," she threatened.

He was still not able to believe his luck. Could it be that the love of his life was talking with the killer of her father? Maybe.

He didn't know what to say. The angel dashed inside. *'This can't happen to me,'* he thought.

He dropped on to his knees, almost on the verge of weeping. His senses had stopped working completely. Police would be arriving any minute. The one girl he loved was the daughter of the man he had killed just now. Life again had played a cruel joke on him. He noticed a man in uniform approaching.

"Vimarsh…Vimarsh…Vimarsh…VIMARSH."

Vimarsh wondered how the investigator knew his name. He was being shaken rudely.

"Vimarsh…you fuckin idiot."

He had fallen into a dark pit.

"You slept the whole day, you fuckin idiot," Nick said, shaking him.

Vimarsh looked confused but relieved. His eyes searched for the package and found it where he had kept it.

He looked at Nick, with relief in his eyes, for the first time.

25

Vimarsh was getting ready for office. He could not keep hiding in the room any more. He kept the package in his bag, which he used to carry to office. He sat on the last seat of the bus and tore open the package. A letter fell out from it along with a photo. He opened the letter first to avoid the same fate as was in his dream.

Vimarsh,

I know you would have found my condition, of killing someone in lieu of your new life amusing.

When I saw you for the first time, you reminded me of myself ten years back. I have covered a lot of ground since that position to reach today's position. Initially I didn't have anyone to guide me but you are not that unlucky as I was. I wanted you to sweat as much as I had toiled in those ten years but you are already three-weeks more experienced than I was.

I hope once you see the photo after reading this letter, it would become clear why I wanted you to eliminate the subject (I love using this 'subject' word).

Once again, I wish you all the best in your new life.
Regards,
Chris

Vimarsh's curiosity was now at its height. He, finally, took out the photograph from the envelope. On glancing at it, he laughed and laughed till his stomach began to hurt.

He noticed the other passengers look at him with anger and surprise but he didn't care.

❦

The city had never looked so pleasant to Vimarsh. The greenery on his route to office, the people he used to be scared off – Vishvesh, Sankat, Nick – all now looked so amusing and childish. What sort of a life had he lived till now?

"Big Bazaar stop."

Vimarsh's train of thoughts came to an abrupt halt.

It was time to exercise control.

❦

He stopped at the office entrance. A human corpse obstructed his way with his back facing Vimarsh. He looked at it and then looked sideways. No one gave any significance to it.

A dead body lay at the office entrance and no one cared. He bent lower and turned it over.

A familiar face confronted him. He rubbed his eyes and a long lost smile came to his face.

'Vimarsh, as everyone had known till now, has finally succumbed to the pressures and departed from his lifeless life.' His dead body now faces Vimarsh.

The man in the photograph had finally been eradicated like an insect. Vimarsh had, at last, fulfilled his promise which he had made to Chris.

26

"Came back? So soon?" Lingasamy greeted Vimarsh. His eyes fixed on the new intern's plunging neckline.

Vimarsh stopped right in front of him, acting as a curtain before his inspecting eyes. Lingasamy was forced to shift his gaze within seconds. "What happened…Vimar…," Lingasamy began as a lump arose in his throat due to the intense stare.

"Sir!" Vimarsh said, with an unruffled decisiveness.

"Sir?"

"Good morning, Vimarsh sir. *Say it.*"

"Ahhh…ummm," Samy seemed on the verge of collapsing.

"Uh huh…say it…Good morning, Vimarsh sir," Vimarsh repeated in the same undertone.

"Good morning…Vimarsh…SIR!" Lingasamy said, stepping back, swallowing the lump in his throat.

"Good morning," Vimarsh replied with a courteous smile. "Is my desk ready?"

Lingasamy looked more than shocked, more at his own behaviour than at the person who stood in front of him.

"Sir, it is not…just wait a second," Lingasamy said, taking almost a minute to realise what should be his next act.

Lingasamy called the sweeper and instructed him about something in his native language in a rather terse tone. The sweeper, without taking an extra minute, magically appeared with a cleaning cloth.

"Sir, your place is ready," Lingasamy said, appearing in front of Vimarsh, looking visibly nervous.

"Good work Samy, thank you," Vimarsh acknowledged. "Keep this and from next time…" he said and handed a fifty-rupee bill to Lingasamy while leaving his sentence hanging in mid air.

A broad smile replaced the nervousness on Lingasamy's face. "Sorry sir, it won't happen again," Samy said, taking the money promptly before Vimarsh changed his mind.

"Who is she?"

"Sir, she is a new intern who joined last to last Thursday along with one more intern. Right now both of them are working under Sankat sir."

"Anything else I should know about her?" Vimarsh asked, handing a crisp twenty-rupee bill to Lingasamy.

"She is from Nagpur. Her father is a professor in some university and mother is a housewife. She has one more sister who is married and lives at BTM. She herself lives near Domlur overbridge in a flat, with her two friends. She does not have any boyfriends," Lingasamy said, trying to regain his breath.

"Keep this and have something good for lunch today and one more thing, the next time if I catch you looking at her in such a manner…," Vimarsh handed him the last ten rupees of the day.

"Sir, I swear to God, it won't happen again, I will bring you coffee."

"Here is the money."

"Don't worry sir, I will adjust it in office account."

'Greenery does increase the speed,' Vimarsh thought. He had started on a triumphant note. He softly stroked the crease of his double breasted suit. It was now time to conquer the next frontier but before that…

༄☙ཎ

"Hi," Vimarsh greeted.

"Hello," Shaila replied, looking rather pensive.

"I think we have not yet met. I am Vimarsh," he said.

"I am Shaila," she replied with a forced smile.

"Nice to meet you, Shaila. So when did you join?"

"Sir…22nd was my first day."

"Welcome to our new family. By the way, who are you reporting to right now?"

"To Sankat sir."

"Not looking very happy though."

"Nothing sir…It is only due to work pressure."

"Doesn't look like it though. If you have any problem, you can come to me…I am Sankat's BOSS."

"Sure sir," Shaila said, brightening up a bit.

"And one more thing, in this office we follow the open-door policy, so nobody is sir or ma'am here. Call everyone with his or her name…so, I am Vimarsh."

"Oh! Okay sir…I mean Vimarsh."

"Okay then…see you soon," Vimarsh said and stood up.

"Vimarsh…actually…," Shaila stopped midway.

"You can trust me if you want to talk about it. It will remain between you and me."

"Well…actually I don't know how to say it. It might be my imagination or maybe I am thinking too much."

"It is okay to think too much sometimes or you might be guessing the situation correctly," Vimarsh responded.

"Maybe…maybe not! I don't know," Shaila said, still lost in thoughts.

"Excuse me sir," Samy came and stood with a plate in his hand.

"Thanks Samy," Vimarsh said.

"Anything else you need…sir," Samy said, looking eager to serve. Had Vimarsh asked him for his hand, he would not have hesitated to chop and give it the next second.

"Do you need anything?" Vimarsh asked Shaila.

"No thanks, I had my breakfast," said Shaila, showing signs of admiration for Vimarsh.

"Okay Samy, thanks," Vimarsh said.

"I have never seen Lingasamy treating anyone with so much respect in this office as he is doing to you; not even Vishvesh sir," Shaila said, looking awestruck.

"I don't know. Never noticed it before today," his smile deepened. "Anyway, you were about to tell me something."

She didn't think twice this time. "Actually Vimarsh, I think Sankat sir is indulging in regionalism. He has given all the work to me and not to the other intern, who happens to be from his native place. He is even favouring him by providing him with old reports on the basis of which to prepare his own training reports and presentations. There are rumours afloat that only one of us will be given the offer letter to join this company after the training is complete and Sankat sir is already backing him as the most suitable candidate before Vishvesh sir. I am already staying late every day just to keep myself afloat with this heavy workload and now, all these petty office politics. I never knew that office politics could be so dirty and cheap." By the end of it all, she was almost in tears.

"Oh okay, so that is the problem," Vimarsh pondered for a while.

"From now on you will report directly to me," Vimarsh said, after a long pause.

"But Vimarsh…Sankat sir."

"Don't worry, I will talk to Vishvesh."

"Okay Vimarsh," Shaila said, giving a wan smile, though some tears were discernible on her cheeks.

"Okay, see you then. Have a nice day."

"You too Vimarsh," Shaila remarked happily.

"Samy, you are looking worried."

"Do you believe in miracles?"

"No, why?"

"Nothing, just saw one today."

27

"Sir, Vishvesh sir had called you to his cabin," Lingasamy informed Vimarsh.

"Okay, thanks," Vimarsh said.

"Yeah, yeah, come in," Vishvesh said.

"Good morning…Vishvesh."

"Mishter Veemars…I think…after coming back fraam you-err naitive place, you have faargaat something," Vishvesh said sarcastically.

"No Vishvesh, I remember everything. As a matter of fact, I remember it more clearly than ever before."

"Whaat do you mean?"

"As per the office memorandum, it is clearly mentioned in paragraph 19(a), line number 5 that we will follow an open-door policy and generally call people by their names……"

"Aukay, aukay, I do naat waant you-err explanations."

"Vishvesh, as a matter of fact it wasn't that. Anyway, I had delegated the responsibility of preparing the accounts of Comconfy Corporation to Sankat before going on leave."

"But he told me…like…the accounts files are weeth you. That's why I are kaalled you here. Are you shoo-err aar you need something…yenithing to verify?"

"I had sent a mail to you also. I think you might have missed it. Anyway, any other thing you need from me?"

"Ass aff nau, everything is fine may be. I will kaal you when I review the laetest daakyuments."

"One more thing, I had asked Shaila to assist me with the presentation of DTA Corporation. I hope you don't have any problem," Vimarsh said.

"Take whoever you want. I want the presentation to be of very besht caality (best quality) and aask Sankat to get a feel of the presentation so that he can prepare it before the mating. I do naat waant yeni mishtakes," Vishvesh said, looking at Vimarsh. "The presentation is aan the day aafter tomaarro, so complete it by today…maybe…and send me a kaapy so that I can review it."

"I will do it," Vimarsh said.

❧❦❧

'It was never difficult, only I was not sure if it could be done,' Vimarsh thought.

"Hi Vimarsh! When did you come back? Holidays over? So soon!…You could have taken a few more days off. The office was working rather efficiently in your gracious absence…Anyway, nice suit, but you could have bought a new one instead of this," Sankat said, laughing at his own joke.

"Can I please get the statements of Comconfy?"

"Boss had given it to you to complete them, so logically, you must be having them, right?" Sankat asked, smirking again.

"I want the statements of Comconfy on my desk. RIGHT NOW."

"Why are you behaving like a parrot, repeating the same line again and again? I told you the statements must be with you."

"Can you please come here?" Vimarsh said calmly.

"Sure, why not?"

A mail dated almost twenty-five days back lay open on Vimarsh's desktop.

Sankat started reading the mail with a smile but as he neared its end, his smile vanished, giving way to a thin grimace.

"So, now can I have the statements of Comconfy?"

"But Vimarsh…I didn't receive this mail," Sankat stammered.

"Do you want me to search it for you?" Vimarsh offered calmly.

"NO…I mean…I think, I might have missed it," Sankat said, voluntarily moving his hands in a bid to stop Vimarsh from reaching his desk.

"Now can you please answer my question?"

"Vimarsh, give me a few more days. I will definitely complete it by this weekend," Sankat cringed.

"I will complete it, sir."

"I will complete it by this weekend…sir," Sankat mumbled the last word after a short pause.

"I want the statements and the file on my desk by this Friday and no excuses this time. I am sending a mail to you, and a copy of it to Vishvesh, detailing everything I want. Don't forget, I want you to reply it."

"But sir, I said I will do it by this Friday. Then why do you need to inform about it to the boss?" Sankat said, sweating like a pig.

"Sankat, it is part of the process. I am just following the rules here…as you fondly call them – the rules of the ring. And can you please send Shaila? I need her to assist me in something."

"But sir, I am her supervisor. And I have already assigned her some work to complete by this Friday."

"I had already informed Vishvesh that from now onwards, Shaila will work under my supervision. If you have any problem with this arrangement, you can talk to Vishvesh."

"No…why should I have any problem, sir?" Sankat said.

"Good, then send her immediately," Vimarsh said, immersing himself in a file.

"Wow!"

"Oh sorry, I didn't notice that I am not alone over here," Vimarsh said, stopping midway. It was six in the evening and the office was almost deserted.

"So you are still in office?" Shaila commented.

"Only when I am in my special mood swings."

"So which way is your mood swinging today?"

"Well, towards happiness and liberation."

"Mine too," Shaila exclaimed. "Oh sorry, am I talking too much?"

"Somewhat. So why are you happy? Any special reason?"

"Actually, I wanted to thank you."

"Precisely, for what?"

"For saving me…I mean I don't want to criticise anyone. Please don't take it amiss…"

"I know what you mean to say. Don't worry, I am not going to tell anything to anyone in the office," Vimarsh said calmly.

"You are different…I mean it in a good sense."

"Don't you think that this is too much over the top, considering that this is only our second meeting?"

"Well, that is one way of looking at it but you can look at it in a different way also."

"In which way?"

"Well I have this special knack for figuring out good people among the lot."

"So you think I am good?"

"Yes, off course," Shaila chuckled.

"I guess you have grossly overestimated me. It would be better if we were to remain aloof at the personal level."

"Well, you are strange, for one thing. But still I am prepared to take this risk," Shaila said, extending her hand.

"Shaila, thanks. But I think we need some more time. You are great but I don't think I am good enough to be your friend, so let's give this some more time."

"Okay…," Shaila said, shocked for a moment. "I can live with that kind of a diplomatic rejection."

Vimarsh smiled, "Should we leave now? I think this presentation is almost complete."

"Okay, as you say."

"Let me send it to Vishvesh and then we can leave," Vimarsh said.

"Okay boss," Shaila giggled.

❦

"Hi!" Vimarsh said excitedly.

"Hello Vimarsh. How was your first day in office?" Chris asked.

"Oh…h it was extraordinary! Never felt so much in control of my life. Chris, I can't thank you enough."

"Not so soon, my friend. You have still not achieved your objective. So maintain your focus."

"I will Chris, I will."

"Good luck, my friend. Success will soon be yours."

❧❀❧

"Good morning, sir," Lingasamy greeted Vimarsh.

"Good morning!"

"Excuse me, Vimarsh sir, I want talk to you about something important," Sankat said as Vimarsh settled down in his chair.

"Yeah, tell me Sankat. Actually I also wanted to talk to you about something. Anyway, shoot." Vimarsh replied.

"Actually sir, the statements are not yet ready. I need more time."

"More time?" he thought for a moment before saying, "Okay send me a mail stating your reasons."

"But sir…"

"Yes Sankat, any problem?"

"No sir…you wanted to talk about something?"

"Oh yes…yes…Vishvesh has told me that we have to make a presentation to a very important client. He wants you to present it. Prepare it well. The meeting is today at ten," Vimarsh said.

"But sir…how can I prepare it in one hour? I mean I have to complete these statements by the end of the day," Sankat said, almost mumbling.

"If you won't give the presentation, then who else will?"

"But sir, you know my situation. I won't be able to do it," Sankat said, trying to give a forced smile.

"Don't worry. Vishvesh will definitely understand."

❧❀❧

"Vishvesh, can I have a word with you?"

"Veemars, I am very busy at this time. The mating is about to start and I just gaat the information that Javier sir is aalso coming to attend this mating. He might be arriving in a few minutes. It will be better if you come laettron with your petty praablems."

"Sankat will not be able to give the presentation," Vimarsh blurted out.

"WHAAT? But why? And why are naat you…like…told me this before," Vishvesh was baffled at the sudden turn of events.

"I was trying to tell you this since the morning but you were not accessible."

"Nau whaat will we do?" Vishvesh's face turned white.

"Hello Vishvesh," a new voice echoed in the environment.

"Good maarning…sir…hau aar you?" Vishvesh tried to gulp his tension.

"I am fine…and how are you…"

"Vimarsh," Vimarsh completed the sentence.

"Oh yes, Vimarsh. Have we met before?"

"I don't think so, sir," Vimarsh said, vividly recalling his last embarrassing rendezvous with Javier.

"That's why I was thinking how I could forget your name. Not my habit, you know," Javier said, basking in his own glory.

Vimarsh chose to say nothing while Vishvesh tried to regroup his thoughts.

"So Vishvesh…," Javier began, shifting his gaze to Vishvesh, "what about the presentation? Who is going to deliver it and where is Sankat?"

"Sir, this time it izz Veemars who will present it," Vishvesh said, trying to avoid Vimarsh's gaze. Vimarsh tried to look shocked at the sudden turn of the events.

"Vimarsh?" Javier tried to recall the face behind this name, "Oh… hh, you mean him? Good luck, gentleman. You better be good since it is very important for our company to build this relationship. I think Vishvesh must have done a lot of thinking before giving the baton to you since he knows how important this is for us and especially for me," Javier said, sounding as if threatening.

Vishvesh turned pale as the light in Javier's eyes changed. He could see that his days in this company were far and few. Vimarsh had never gone on the stage; not even to adjust the microphone, and here the most important presentation of Vishvesh's life was…

"Sir, the clients have arrived at the reception," the receptionist announced.

"Let's go Vishvesh. All the best Vimarsh," Javier said, leading the way. Vishvesh followed.

29

"Good maarning, gentlemen," Vishvesh cleared his throat. "You are already meet Mishter Javier, the Vice President of our company."

Javier nodded his head in greeting.

The room was filled with four odd-looking fat men from the client company. The look on their faces was grim and clearly revealed that they were not at all happy to come and meet Javier and Vishvesh. The one who looked a bit older than the other three cleared his throat after greeting Javier, "Mr Vishvesh, can we directly move to the proceedings since we don't have much time?"

His curt statement wiped the forced smile on Vishvesh's face, "Yeah sure. Vimarsh, are you ready?" Javier said, taking control of the situation before it went out of hand since Vishvesh looked as if his soul had been sucked out from his body.

"Sure Javier," Vimarsh said.

Javier saw red at the absence of the word 'sir' but said nothing.

"Good morning, gentleman," Vimarsh began, looking unperturbed at the looks on the faces of Javier and Vishvesh. "We have studied your balance sheets of the last ten years of your profit and loss statements and after doing an extensive research and study, we have reached at some definite conclusions." Vimarsh then glanced at the four pairs of foreign eyes. They were listening with rapt attention.

"But before moving on further, we would like you to help us so that we can assist you in a better way," Vimarsh paused. The expressions in the four pairs of eyes changed from attention to curiosity.

Vishvesh feared his end was near.

"Actually we need to know what you want us to assist you with? I mean, how can we provide high value service to your company?"

"Young man," the oldest of the lot again started on a terse note. It was now Javier's turn to turn pale. *'This meeting is going down to hell, I must do something. This is not the way to conduct such an important presentation,'* Javier thought in that split second.

"…I don't know what to say…," the old man continued as Vimarsh's stomach took a somersault, "…except one thing, that this is the best question I have ever heard in my twenty years of career. Yours is the first company which really wants to know our requirements unlike others, who give us cheap presentations about their past achievements and non-feasible solutions to our non-existent problems. Please let us know what you want to know about us. We would be happy to answer." A smile on his face ended the drought of warmth in the room.

༶❀༶

Forty minutes went flying in the midst of queries and suggestions.

"Congrats young man! Your ideas will definitely help us. We are looking forward to this alliance," said the old man and shook hands with Vimarsh. The meeting ended on a pleasant note.

Javier stood behind Vimarsh, displaying a broad smile.

Vishvesh tried to smile but the end result was a mixture of confusion, uncertainty and fear.

"I hope the same sincerity that you displayed today will be evident in our association when you handle this project for us. Am I right Javier?"

"Absolutely, Mr Khanna." At that moment had Mr Khanna asked for his kidneys or liver, Javier would have smilingly obliged.

A slew of handshakes were accomplished in a matter of seconds.

༶❀༶

"Congrats Vimarsh," Shaila approached Vimarsh as he settled down in his place. Javier led the consortium for lunch to a posh restaurant. Vishvesh decided to stay back for some strange reasons – strange because he never let go of anything on company's expenses, be it food, stationery or even toilet paper.

"I heard you gave a dashing presentation in front of the clients," Shaila chuckled.

"Never ever heard such things about myself. It will be better if you don't believe such rumours," Vimarsh replied.

"Veemars can I taalk to you faar five minutes?" Vishvesh came out from his royal cabin to meet the lesser mortals of his office, something that he had never done since he became the manager three years back. It was like an era coming to an end and paving the way for a new one.

"Yeah sure! Just give me a few moments, I will join you soon," Vimarsh said.

"Vimarsh sir, something serious, *kya*? Vishvesh sir was asking about your seating place. I think something serious happened and that's why he came out from his cabin," Samy said, looking worried.

"Don't know Samy. Let's see," Vimarsh tried to parry all the unwanted attention he was getting from the rest of the office.

"Today this sucker will be gone forever," Sankat muttered under his breath.

"He must have done something radical to be summoned by the boss himself," another whispered.

Shaila looked worried.

Sheena looked impressed for strange reasons known only to her.

"What might be the reason, Vimarsh?" Shaila asked.

"Don't know. Can't say anything right now," Vimarsh said, going towards Vishvesh's cabin.

30

"Yes Vishvesh, tell me."

Vishvesh was deep in thought when Vimarsh's polite voice woke him up.

"Yeah, yeah, Veemars, please have a seat," welcomed Vishvesh.

Vimarsh's senses reeled from anxiety. He sat down on the edge of the chair.

"Hau aar you feeling nau after such a nice presentation?"

"Good."

"You are woked hoard faar it. I will definitely taalk with Javier sir faar giving you emplaayee aaf the year awaard and aalso a very good increment."

"Thanks, Vishvesh."

"Naat a problem Veemars," Vishvesh said, looking pleased with his own magnanimity. "I aalways think about our emplaayees. You peepul aar my family."

That's why you always treat us like untouchables,' Vimarsh thought.

"Veemars, in the mating, Mr Khanna said that he waants you to lead this praaject…In fact he might reecommend this to Javier sir… you know that the client is a vyery impaartant faar us and considering you-err inexperience I do naat think that you will be able to lead yeni team……but off course Mr Khanna are not knowing this…… but you know that faar the sake aaf this company, we should aalways trust peepul who aar experienced and capable of handling such large accounts…bee-caas if something yenithing goes wraang, whaat other peepul might say? No, no, this should naat be the case. I am not telling that I should be the leader but if the company aasks me for my expertise, I can naat say 'no' since it is for the company to say we wok for and naat for us. You are understanding what I meaning, right?"

Vimarsh nodded his head.

"I will try to convhince Javier sir about this. But if he aasks you faar you-err opinion you know whaat you have to say, right? I mean if I would have been at you-err place I would have said 'no', you know."

"Yeah, Vishvesh I know," Vimarsh replied disinterestedly.

Vishvesh didn't know what to make of Vimarsh's reply; nevertheless he continued.

"Veemars, aukay you can go back at you-err desk. Thanks for understand me. Veemars one more thing…no need to apply faar the leaves which you took in the last three weeks. Consider it as a caamp aff," Vishvesh said with an unwanted smile, revealing his yellow teeth lurking through his bushy moustache. "Veemars, can you prepare a report about the mating today so that we can use it as a case study for the rest of our emplaayees?"

❦

Vimarsh returned to his desk, deep in his thoughts.

"Hello, may I talk to Chris?"

"May I know who is talking?" a sweet voice asked.

"This is Vimarsh."

"Oh hi Vimarsh. This is Malvika. How are you?"

"Hi Malvika! I am fine."

"Actually we are preparing for a party tonight," Malvika announced excitedly.

"Wish I could be there," Vimarsh said, showing his longing.

"Chris," Malvika handed the phone to Chris.

Vimarsh told everything to Chris, who let out a deep sigh!

"If Javier calls you for any discussion, go and listen to him but don't say anything. You are a deserving candidate for the managerial post. In negotiations, *one who speaks first, loses*," Chris said, ending his miniature speech with a Chrisanism.

❦

"Come in Vimarsh," Javier said, sitting at the same place where Vimarsh had sat a while ago, listening to Vishvesh's preaching. Vishvesh was seated on his royal chair, looking more like a goat who was about to be slaughtered. Vimarsh occupied a chair in front of Javier.

"Congratulations for your antics today. The client seems to like it a lot. Though it was different from the usual, I am a believer in new ideas. So I am glad you adopted this new approach."

"Thanks sir," Vimarsh said politely.

"Okay Vimarsh, now the client wants only you to lead this project. I have already discussed the issue with Vishvesh, who too has given some inputs but I want to know your views also. That's why I called you."

Vimarsh said nothing and shifted his gaze from Javier to Vishvesh. Javier shifted uneasily in his chair.

"Vishvesh told me you are a loyal employee of this company since a long time and you avoid limelight. Maybe that's why we have never met and looking at your inexperience in handling the accounts in the past, I think it would be better if someone like Vishvesh were to handle it. You can assist him so that you can learn to handle big projects and since we need people like you in our company to evolve as future leaders. What do you say?"

"Javier, if you want to know my opinion, then I would prefer to handle this account as a lead. And since I have spent a considerable amount under Vishvesh, I am confident that through the assistance of a team of my choice, I can successfully handle this account," Vimarsh said with confidence.

Vishvesh looked at Vimarsh with a feeling of betrayal, disgust and hatred. Javier seemed somewhat confused, unable to decide what to do next.

"Veemars, iph you aasks me then I think that you still need some more experience…like…maybe two or three years before even think-ing about handling this kind of project," Vishvesh said, desperately trying to control the situation.

Vimarsh said nothing. Five more minutes passed and the room buzzed with silence.

"Are you sure?" Javier asked, finally breaking the bone.

"Absolutely," Vimarsh gave a crisp reply.

Javier took a deep breath. The silence seemed deafening for Vishvesh. Vimarsh shifted in his seat to take a more comfortable position.

"Veemars you aar naat understanding the situation," Vishvesh muttered, albeit loudly.

Nothing moved. Vimarsh shifted his gaze from Javier to Vishvesh and back to Javier, who was looking directly at Vimarsh.

'One who speaks first loses,' Chris voice resounded in Vimarsh's head. He smiled.

"Whaat is happening here? Is this some kind of a zoke faar you?" Vishvesh asked, losing his patience with every passing minute.

No one else tried to break the ever-expanding calmness in the room. Seven more minutes passed and Vimarsh was still in no mood to say anything.

"This aafice caant have two managers?" Vishvesh finally blurted out what he hadn't wanted to say.

Vimarsh tried hard not to smile.

"Do you also think the same?" Javier asked, looking at Vimarsh.

"It can, if both are handling different areas," Vimarsh said.

"What will be your area of expertise?"

"Finance," Vimarsh said, without waiting for the question to end.

"Increment?"

"1.5 times more than his salary."

"This is extaartion," Vishvesh intervened.

"Why do you think we are going to pay you that much?"

"I am the only one who can successfully lead this project. You know it and finance is one area where you need one of the smartest people in your company?"

"And you think you are the one?" Javier asked.

"Thinking for such obvious things is a waste of time for both of us."

"What if I refuse?"

"You can refuse, but the point is you still can't refute many other things."

"Like what?" Javier asked, secretly enjoying the verbal duel.

"The way today's presentation went, the way we are talking about things here, the way you and I are confident about my work and the way you and I are sure about achieving success in this project."

"May be, but how does it justify your salary demands?" Javier asked, not yet willing to throw the towel.

"If you are good at something, never do it for free. That is my rule number one," Vimarsh said.

Javier paused for a minute and asked, "What is rule two?"

"Never forget the rule number one."

Vishvesh stared at both of them with incredulity in his eyes. He felt helpless but couldn't help enjoying their duel and eagerly awaited the final outcome.

"What is exactly on your mind?" Javier asked.

"I want a team of my choice and I will report directly to you for any matter. There will be no other intermediate and I would like to sit at the same place where I am seated right now."

"That sounds reasonable but don't you want a new cabin once you become the manager?"

"I have my reasons."

"You are strange for some obvious reasons. You will get your confirmation letter by today evening."

"I look forward to it," Vimarsh said and extended his hand. Javier clasped his hand.

Vishvesh's dream of getting the highest salary package in AKFC and thwart every attempt by anyone to occupy his chair which he used to lovingly call his third love collapsed. He didn't know how it had come about but his tormentor was the one whom he tormented each day.

Vimarsh was surprised at his own reaction at this turn of events. He was least overjoyed at his sudden success; an unusual calmness was visible in his demeanour. If this had happened in his previous life he might have jumped with joy and excitement, but not now.

꧁ꗞꗞ꧂

Vishvesh looked dumbstruck as he stood at the door through which Javier and Vimarsh just walked out.

He hurriedly picked up the phone and said, "I want him in my cabin right now."

"Yes…yes sir," Sankat stammered. He had never heard Vishvesh speak so angrily.

"You wanted to see me?" Vimarsh asked as he peeped in, with his half body leaning almost on the threshold of Vimarsh's cabin's door.

"Yeah, yeah, come," Vishvesh said, trying to control his anger till the door closed. "Sit."

Vimarsh sat without saying anything.

"Whaat do you think you did just nau?"

"I don't get you."

"You know whaat I am taalking about."

"You mean the meeting with Javier?"

"Whaat makes you think that you aar the besht man in the aaffice in finance and administrasion?"

"Is there anyone else better?"

"Do naat taalk to me in that tone. I am naat Javier."

Vimarsh noted the absence of the word 'sir' that generally followed the name Javier and said, "Tell me one name."

"There are many," Vishvesh replied, trembling with rage.

"One name."

"Sankat."

"According to my knowledge, he can't even prepare a balance sheet without making at least a thousand mistakes."

"THAT IS BULLSHIT," Vishvesh roared.

"Don't talk to me like that…ever," Vimarsh threatened, drawing menacingly close to Vishvesh, who looked petrified at the warning.

"Sankat was aalways a better chaaice which you are aalso have noticed," he continued, holding his ground.

"Since the time I remember, Sankat was never a choice. It was I who did all the work, all the files, all the reports and every damn paperwork."

"Hau can you tells such an outrageous caamment?"

"You can check your mail as the proof. I had sent you all the status reports every single day and don't forget to check the time when these mails were sent. You might get proof of my claims."

Vishvesh said nothing for a while. Then he said, "I thaaght you are a laayal and intelligent emplayee. I aalso did favour by approving those caamp aff for you-er leaves."

"Excuse me Vishvesh. Listen to me very carefully *now*. You have not done any favour to me. I deserved what I got because I worked for them. That was my right, so don't give me any lecture on doing me a favour.

"Hau can you taalk like this to me? I thaaght you are such a…" Vishvesh said, trembling with anger. "Is there no way to change you-err decision? You aar naat understanding the respaansibilities coming with this one wraang decision. I am more experienced and trust me I know that the time is not yet right. You aar naat ready and I have planned better things faar you. We can have a mating about you-err new role and repaansibilities, may be tommaro." Vishvesh was now begging.

"Vishvesh, you might not understand what all I have done for this company, and I can totally understand that. Someone who is so obsessed with his designation and cabin can't really see who is devoting time to the job and who is trying to butter up the boss. So stop giving me lectures on favour and calibre…I am done here. Is there anything else you want to say or add?"

He waited for a few seconds but Vishvesh was too shocked to say anything sensible.

"I have mailed you the report you asked for and this time ask Sankat to change the words 'use' to 'utilise', 'money' to 'finance' and 'furniture' to 'physical assets' in the report. I don't have time for such things," said Vimarsh, before marching out of the cabin.

31

"Hey Vimarsh, I am taking your mobile for a few days."

"Where is yours?"

"It is with me."

"So use it."

"We all are going to Goa. My cell has nil balance and since your connection is postpaid, common sense suggests I should take your phone."

"No problem but I need the sim card...you can take the set."

"Joking...hmmm...and that too with your daddy...huh? Hey what is this?" Nick said, looking at the paper which fell from Vimarsh's pocket while taking his mobile out.

"It is for you," Vimarsh handed it to Nick.

"...Total amount...four lakhs, twenty seven thousand, three hundred eighty seven rupees and twenty five paisa," Nick looked at Vimarsh with a baffled expression.

"This is the total amount that I had spent on your rent, mobile bills, food, clothing, movies, disco outings, cigarettes, beer, whisky and your numerous girlfriends whom I had sponsored in these two and a half years. It is inclusive of 10% interest, 10.3% service tax and 13.5% VAT. You have one week at your disposal to give the first installment of this loan, which amounts to fifteen thousand a month till thirty months."

"Ha! Ha! Ha! Ha!" Nick laughed meekly. "Good joke, very good joke...Vimarsh...very good joke. *Yaar*, if you don't want to give your cell, it's okay, no problem at all. I will recharge my mobile."

"Do you really think I am cracking jokes here?" Vimarsh asked, looking as placid as a lake.

"See Vimarsh, neither had I taken any loan from you nor can you force me to shell out anything from my pocket without my will."

"Neither do I intend to do that," Vimarsh said in the same tone.

"Vimarsh, look, we are friends. I mean WE ARE FUCKIN BEST FRIENDS. How can you do this to YOUR best friend?"

"Okay, I have another option if you are prepared for it?"

"Yeah sure. Tell me, my bestest friend," Nick said, feeling relieved.

"You have to do the household chores from now on – all the cleaning, dusting, washing clothes, buying groceries and every other housework."

"WHAT?" Nick was shocked. "Are you out of your mind or what? Do you expect me to do all that, washing clothes and all?"

"Okay, not a problem. Since you are not willing to pay the EMIs nor willing to do the work, the only option is that you better start searching for another abode for yourself."

"Have you gone nuts? You can't tell me what to do or what not to do in my life? You are a born loser…a fuckin born loser. You don't even have any friends except me and you are giving me this crap? Who the hell do you think you are? You think that you can throw me out from here just like that?" Nitin became hysterical.

"Well, first thing first. Stop shouting like a demented person. Second thing, YES, I can throw you out any time I want. You might have forgotten it but I want to remind you that this house's lease is in my name. You are only a guest here. Moreover, all this while it was I who was paying the rent, so I don't need you anyway. Starting from tomorrow morning, you have five days in hand to find another place. I am off to bed now and may you have a peaceful night."

"But Vimarsh, this isn't over. I need to talk about this NOW," Nitin's voice rose higher with frustration as the door closed behind Vimarsh.

Various expletives could be heard rising from the hall long after the conversation was over.

꧁꧂

"Good morning, sir," Sankat greeted eagerly.

"Good morning, Sankat," Vimarsh hid his astonishment beneath his smile.

"Sir, many congratulations for your promotion."

"Thanks, Sankat."

"Sir, I want to offer my assistance in choosing your new team."

"Thanks Sankat. I will take a decision on the team soon," Vimarsh smiled.

"I also wanted to let you know that I am ready to play any possible role in the team."

"I will definitely think about it and let you know," Vimarsh said with a wide grin.

～◎◇～

"Hi Vimarsh! Looking fab today," Sheena winked at him.

"Thanks for the compliment," Vimarsh said as he weaved his way towards his desk.

"Congrats on your promotion. Never saw such quick rise in our sweet little family," Sheena said with a hint of jealousy in her voice.

"Thank you but you can look at yourself once in a while to find the answers to such questions," Vimarsh said, pointing obliquely at Sheena's three promotious in the last two years.

"I guess that is a compliment."

"It is, of course."

"I heard you are about to choose a new team for your new assignment."

"I will take a decision in that regard in the coming two or three days," Vimarsh said, trying to shrug off the topic. He wanted seclusion while choosing his team.

"I just wanted to let you know that I am available whenever you want...I mean, for this new assignment," Sheena said with a naughty smile at him.

"You bet...I definitely will," Vimarsh gave her a thumbs-up with a quick smile.

～◎◇～

Vimarsh chose five lesser known mortals of the office in his team, including Shaila. It was quite a raw, inexperienced team in every respect.

Javier didn't question his decision but Vishvesh did and so did Sheena.

～◎◇～

"What interests you in her?"

"What interests you in my interest?" Vimarsh shot back.

"Just curious about your choice of her in your team when you have better options. Are you one of those who thinks a woman to be a beautiful object rather than a purposeful pursuit?"

"Why does it bother you what I think about women? More so, since you are not my type."

"Smart?"

"Single."

"So my singleton status makes you wary and nervous," Sheena said, in no mood to leave Vimarsh in solitude.

"You bet."

Sheena laughed heartily.

Vimarsh said nothing. The discussion was already over for him.

Sheena looked at him again with a defeated look and left for her desk.

❧

"Sir, you called me?"

"Come inside."

Vishvesh closed the door slowly behind Sankat as he entered the room. Sankat knew what was coming. "You really disappointed me Sankat. I do naat know hau difficult it was to convince him to take you in his team. If you had done full attempt, you are in his team by nau."

Sankat said nothing.

"Nau I have to think of other ways to know what he is up to," Vishvesh blabbered with his back towards him.

"Sir, if you concentrate on your team than his team, I think it will benefit all of us." Vishvesh turned back, astounded at the bold reply and turned to glare at Sankat but the latter had already left the room.

❧

Working under Vishvesh was a learning experience for Vimarsh as he had come to realise why some of the previous clients had left AKFC for some lesser known companies. So his first area of concern was to get rid of bureaucracy, beginning with his team.

"Hello guys and gals," Vimarsh greeted when conducting his first meeting with his team.

Everyone was amazed at the frank demeanour of their new leader.

"Before beginning the meeting, we must find out why we are here. Agenda for today: if someone feels that he or she has already thorough knowledge about the topics here, he or she can go back to his or her work. My aim is to maximise the benefits of these meetings while saving on time and don't think anyone will feel bad if you were not to attend any of these. I leave this decision entirely on you. If there is some important meeting which I want all of you to attend, I will let you know in advance. Is this clear to you?"

Everyone nodded their heads in unison.

Vimarsh presented the agenda.

"First thing first. Since we are six persons in all, it amounts to six equally capable brains. So I need you all to toss up any idea, however small it is, in front of the team. If found feasible, it will be implemented and due credit given to the concerned person. Is that okay with you all?"

"That will be a valuable chance to experiment with the new trends in the industry," Pratyush said enthusiastically.

"For me, you guys will be everything. The client comes second. So, if you face any problem of any kind, you can come to me at any time. You can come even if the problem is purely personal and you want to discuss it."

Everyone looked more than amused, because so many good things could never be true at the same time.

"Also, one last thing. I am not someone who knows everything about everything but I am open to learning new things and I would appreciate it if you too give priority to learning over your procrastinating nature, be it in any field. So if you know something which is not in my knowledge, I would be pleased to learn it from you. We are still in talks with the client about his expectations from us. Once it is finalised, I will toss the roles and their descriptions for you to choose your role. I won't assign anyone any role, since I want you guys to choose the role best suited to your capabilities and interests. That is all from my side. If you have any queries, then you are free to ask."

Vimarsh concluded his first meeting on a triumphant note. Everyone seemed eager to jump start on his or her tasks.

"Vimarsh sir, can you tell us briefly about the project and the client?" one of the team members asked.

"I am glad you asked this question. And one more thing, my name is Vimarsh and not Vimarsh sir as I am in no mood to change it. So please call me by my real name," Vimarsh said, smiling.

∽◌ઈ

"Vimarsh, Javier sir has sent a memo to our team, which I think we need to discuss."

"I know Shaila, I was about to call a meeting."

Everyone was tense at getting a memo from Javier on the second day itself. The memo read:

"This is a very important client for us and hence I expect you all to give your 200 per cent to this project. I would like to stress on some major points so that you can work together more cohesively. Consider this as a regular practice from now on. This change, by all means, will allow us to leverage better our talent base in an area where developmental roles are underway and strategically take us towards the upcoming business system transition where systems literacy and accuracy will be noteworthy in maintaining and to further improve service levels for our customer base."

It was followed by a presentation on the strategy.

"Vimarsh, I didn't understand a word of it," spoke out one of the young teammates.

"It simply means that since this is a very important client for us, he expects us to give your 200 per cent to this project. This change, by all means, will allow us to better leverage our talent base in an area where developmental roles are underway and strategically focuses us towards the upcoming Business system transition where systems literacy and accuracy will be prominent and noteworthy in maintain-

ing and to further improve services to our levels to our customers base
forward. Now let's get on with the presentation."

෴

"Veemars, where are you going?" Vishvesh asked while waiting for the
bus and standing near Vimarsh.
    "In that bus."
    "No no, we won't go in that bus."
    "Why? What is the problem?"
    "That intern is getting into that bus *naa*. Now we are equals and
you must know that managers do naat travel with their subaardinates,"
Vishvesh said, pointing at Shaila who was gesturing to Vimarsh to get
into the bus.
    "Some other day Vishvesh…some other day…when I will think
on this point," Vimarsh said hastily while jumping into the bus which
had started moving.

෴

"What was he saying?" Shaila asked as soon as Vimarsh came and sat
down next to her.
    "As usual, giving me a crash course on the behaviour of a
manager."
    "Asshole," Shaila exploded.
    "Chill; it's not important."
    "Anyway, today you rocked in the meeting. Everyone was talking
about you. Even the guys from the other teams were surprised to learn
about your knowledge on management. *Accha,* I have one small query.
Why did you choose me in your team?" Shaila asked impatiently.
    "Why means?"
    "I mean why did you choose me in your team…as simple as that,"
Shaila repeated her question with her large kohl-lined eyes fixed on
Vimarsh.
    "What do you think?"

"I don't know. May be because you think you are my saviour or may be because you like me or may be because there was no other choice, so you played safe."

"Can I use my lifeline?" he grinned.

"You don't have any left in your kitty. Answer me."

"It is neither of these. Actually I am a fan of James Bond movies and you look like Sean Connery." The reply was given with a poker face.

"What a nice joke!" Shaila said.

The bus took a turn from Kundallahalli gate towards Marathahalli Bridge.

"Where do you stay?" Shaila fired another one.

"Were you born with a quiz book?" Vimarsh asked.

"Don't remember such tiny details…where do you stay?"

"Sorry, but I don't remember such tiny details," Vimarsh replied.

"You are a smart ass, aren't you?"

"*Oye,* I am your team lead."

"So what? You are my friend first and I can tell my friends anything I want," Shaila replied with her chin up.

"Is that so? But we are still not friends. You remember our deal?"

"So what? I consider you as my friend. It is a one-sided friendship at the moment."

"What is this one-sided friendship? I have heard only about one-sided love."

"One-sided friendship means that one can do anything for the other person without expecting any return."

Some emotions arose in his chest, reminding him of his previous life. He smiled at the unusual ease with which Shaila had come to regard him as her friend.

32

It had been almost two weeks since Vimarsh had seen her. His main assessment still awaited him; he was busy with his new responsibilities and still his mind often drifted towards her.

He still remembered her smiling face which he saw last in the same bus in which he travelled every day with the hope of seeing her again.

Though depressed, he saw a glimmer of hope that when she would appear in front of him, he would be able to restore his calm and cool.

'May God bless me,' he thought.

It was Wednesday and Vimarsh boarded the bus with the hope of seeing her. After buying a ticket for ITPL, Vimarsh was lost in his thoughts when a tinkling voice broke his reverie. Dressed in a mint green top and smoky brown trousers, her eyes invited Vimarsh to talk to her but something inside him made him wait.

"Change *illa*," the conductor said in a rude tone.

"Just see, *bhaiya*, you might get it from somebody," she said in a worried tone, feeling uncomfortable at being ridiculed in front of so many people.

"It is not my job to get the change for every Aishwarya Rai. If you didn't have change, you shouldn't have entered," the conductor said, enjoying the slaughter of pretty eyes in which tears had welled up by now.

"What happened?" Vimarsh asked, placing his hand of authority on the shoulder of the conductor.

"It does not concern you."

"What is your name?"

"Why?" the conductor turned his gun at Vimarsh.

"Your name?"

"Hallapa," he said though signs of apprehension were apparent on the conductor's face.

"Hallapa, two options – either apologise to her or a complaint against you will be lodged at the BMTC office."

"Do whatever you want. I face these things daily. I have not done anything wrong," Hallapa retorted.

"Actually you are right. My complaint won't be that effective, but if three passengers complain against you, then it might carry some weight, isn't it? Aunty, won't you raise your voice against this kind of behaviour as tomorrow it might happen to you also?" Vimarsh asked the lady sitting right besides the victim.

The lady looked surprised at the sudden question. Everyone else turned to look at her, waiting for her response.

"You are right son. We pay for the ticket, so why should we face such rude behaviour. I will complain against him," she said, recovering soon from the question.

"I will also complain against him," one more lady sitting at the back seat joined in.

Soon everyone was eager to jump on the bandwagon. It was turning into a match of one against seventy frustrated passengers. The conductor had already lost colour from his face.

"You still have the first option open," Vimarsh prodded, looking at the conductor.

"I am so…sor…sorry, madam, I should not have talked to you like this," Hallapa said.

A round of applause followed.

॰ೱ॰

Vimarsh didn't feel the need to go back to his place. In any case, it was already occupied by somebody. She looked at him with gratitude in her eyes.

"Next stop, Vydehi Hospital."

Her neighbour got up. A slight head nod from her signalled to Vimarsh to grab the chance to sit beside her.

"Hi, I am Ramita."

"I am Vimarsh."

"So, what else do you do apart from intimidating the conductors?"

Vimarsh smiled, "I think for the first meeting this much information is enough. Rest we can discuss over a cup of coffee." Rule number four.

Ramita was surprised at the sudden withdrawal by Vimarsh from the game. She however, gave her mysterious smile.

"What makes you think that I would like to meet you again?"

"I don't believe in destiny but my fair guess is we will meet soon and it will be you who will decide to contact me," Vimarsh said, taking a blank paper out from his pocket. "Here is my e-mail id. Send me the message when you are ready with the place where we can have coffee."

"E-mail id? So you consider yourself a tech wizard?"

"I could be anything but that. But I don't want you to disturb me by calling me when I am in some important meeting or during odd times."

"Why are you so cocky?"

"Meet you soon, 'bye," Vimarsh said and got down from the bus. He somehow resisted looking at her from outside. He knew her eyes were fixed on him.

SCORE: Vimarsh=1, Ramita=0.

෴

"Shaila, will you accompany me for coffee?" A week later Vimarsh found himself asking this question. An e-mail from Ramita had prompted him to take quick action.

The main line hinted to him that Ramita had long resisted the idea of meeting him.

"I just want to return the favour you did for me in the bus. That's why I am sending you this mail."

But it did set the mood for the meeting. Doing a favour had proved an effective arrow in his armour that now provided him the edge. Vimarsh thanked the one who invented it.

It was highly unlikely that she would come alone, he knew. So he needed someone to be his Man Friday. In the worse case, if Ramita came alone, she would at least get the hint that Vimarsh was not needy.

"Today? What time?" Shaila's eyes were fixed on Vimarsh in the hope of getting more details.

"Six."

"What's her name?"

"Anonymous."

'How did she know?' he wondered.

Shaila burst into loud laughter while he heaved a sigh of relief that Shaila had agreed to come. He felt a pang of guilt for using Shaila to serve a personal purpose but shrugged the whole idea away, soon.

༄◉༄

"Quite a crowd today."

"Friday, Vimarsh…Friday."

"Hmmm."

"Should we sit here?"

"As you say," Vimarsh said, his eyes searching for someone.

༄◉༄

"Hello," a sweet voice startled them.

He quickly turned back.

"Hi," Shaila greeted in return with a curious look.

"Hello," a male voice greeted Vimarsh and Shaila alike.

"H…hello."

"This is Anchit," Ramita introduced Anchit to them.

"This is Shaila. Shaila, this is Ramita," Vimarsh said, feeling relieved.

He had suspected that Ramita wouldn't come alone but he had not expected such a towering personality to accompany her in the second meeting.

༄◉༄

"So, you both work in the same office?" Vimarsh fired his first.

"You can say so but until she fell in love with me, I was almost non-existent for her," Anchit said, casting a lovey-dovey look at Ramita.

"You seem disturbed, something wrong?" Ramita asked teasingly,

"Actually I was thinking how such a smart guy could be your boyfriend," Vimarsh replied nonchalantly.

'How could he reach this assumption when she could be hounded by several men and one of them could actually be her boyfriend?'

"It is all luck."

"I guess so. So, Anchit, what do you do?"

Anchit smiled slightly, "I work as a business analyst who is proud to say that he has accomplished almost everything one can dream of in a small period of four years. You know, when I joined office four years back, the systems were quite disorganised; actually there were no systems in place. I had to slog hard to put everything in its proper place."

Shaila yawned sheepishly, while something came to Vimarsh's mind as the clock struck 7.

"Shaila, aren't you getting late?" Vimarsh asked, winking at her.

"Actually I am."

"Hey, Anchit I am sorry but we have to leave."

"Sure…hey, may I know your full name?" Anchit asked, looking rather sad and pensive.

"Vimarsh…Vimarsh Kant Chaturvedi," Vimarsh replied.

"You have a rather long and funny name," Anchit said, trying not to smile too much. "Here is my number. Give me a call sometime," Anchit added in a bid to mend the bridges.

Vimarsh replied, "I only give calls to pretty ladies and I don't think you are anywhere near."

Shaila giggled. Ramita looked sideways, smiling though.

"Anyway, why don't you come to the bowling alley at M.G. Road sometime? This weekend we are going there, I mean Ramita and some of our friends," Anchit said, somewhat discomfited.

Vimarsh now looked clueless. Bowling was just an another fancy name to his ears.

"What happened? Are you worried that your small tummy might be a hindrance in playing?" Ramita said, enjoying every moment of it.

"On the contrary, I was thinking if Anchit could spare some time to give me some tips on improving my bowling skill. What do you say, Anchit?"

"Sure, why not?"

"Okay then, meet you on this weekend," Vimarsh said.

The proceedings in the last one hour had almost thrown a spanner in his works. The discovery of Anchit as Ramita's boyfriend had caught Vimarsh completely on the wrong foot.

SCORE: Vimarsh=1, Ramita=1.

Part V
Anchit Saxena

33

4th April 2006, Indian Institute of Management, Ahmedabad

"...Leadership is neither a science nor an art; it is plain common sense with a sense of service. When you set aside your ego and look for qualities in people which you yourself don't possess, when you hire talent and not the person, when you are able to hire the people who are smarter than you and retain them too, then my friend, you can call yourself a true servant and a visionary."

Sameer Bhatia ended his speech with a sweeping gesture from his hand like a casual wave in the air. The hall erupted in a loud applause that was both in approval and appreciation.

Sameer Bhatia, the founder of Silicon Valley's one of the largest dotcom companies in a matter of two years. He was 6"2' with a robust built, encased in a Valentino suit. He demeanour was polished and air...arrogant. He descended the stairs in a calculated manner that was in perfect sync with his stature. His company had just opened a new office in India and he wanted only the best for it and what else could be a better place than an IIM to scout for such talent.

~❦~

Anchit Saxena was feeling like a hall of fame.

He had received an offer letter from the most happening company of Silicon Valley and a pay package to die for. Only one thing which worried him was his posting in Bangalore.

"Beta, don't worry, I will shift there as soon as you want me to be there," his mother consoled him. "I also have to look after this house. There is no one whom I can trust here."

"Maa, I don't want to go there. I don't care about money or status. I and my two friends are planning to start a company of our own. It can

function from here also. I don't want to join a big company where there won't be any place for my dreams."

"If you have already decided to ditch Sameer Bhatia's offer for some dream that you are spinning, then who am I to advise you? A mother can only wish her son all the best in his endeavours."

"*Maa,* I know you want me to join that company but I also have a dream to start a company like that some day."

"If you have already decided, then I have no other option but to be happy for you. Don't worry about the offer. They might choose someone else. Who was the second best student after you? Yes, Prem. They might choose him instead of you."

"Prem…no. They won't choose him again…they rejected him once. How can they choose him now?"

"Off course, they will choose him. Who else is so brilliant and efficient to replace you, except him?"

"No please, don't say this. I can see anyone there but him."

"Who am I to tell you a lie? The truth will come forward in a matter of weeks."

"I still won't join the company."

"No one can force you to do what you don't wish to do."

"I love you, *Maa.* Thanks for understanding," Anchit said, still not sure whether he was right or not.

"I love you my child in spite of…I am happy that you will be here with me till my last breath, in this small house."

"Don't worry, *Maa,* it is only a matter of few years. Then we will also be living in a comfortable house."

༄༅༅

Anchit was proud about his package which, was twenty-five with five zeroes added. He was smart, dynamic, always well dressed and fiercely competitive. His stature in office complemented his personality and his IIM education. He acted like a superstar in his office and his athletic body and good sports skills only served to add to his stature.

And he did join the company of Sameer Bhatia. His dream could still wait. Prem did start a company though, in the rural area of north India.

34

"So you love her?" Shaila asked as they sat down in the bus after having coffee with Ramita and Anchit,

"Whom?"

"You know what I am talking about!"

"I really don't know what you are talking about," he was in no mood to fall in the trap.

"Ramita. You like her, don't you?"

"Who told you that?"

"The way you kept looking at her and the expression on your face when she introduced you to Anchit were enough."

"Oh…then I am not a good actor."

"So you like her?"

"You are telling me or plainly asking?"

"You can contemplate whatever you want."

"You are smart though you don't look like one."

"Thank you for your unassuming praise."

❦

"Why did you invite him?"

"I guess I invited both of them."

"Whatever…but why?"

"Why are you so disturbed?"

"I don't like him," Ramita complained.

"I thought you liked him and that's why we went to meet them," Anchit said, looking baffled.

"It was something else. You won't understand."

"Maybe since IIMs do not teach us girl psychology."

"I am not in the mood of taking your IIM jokes. Drop me at my apartment," she chided.

Anchit occasionally kept glancing at Ramita but she said nothing during the rest of the journey.

༺ঔ৶

"You still haven't answered my question?"

"I don't feel the need."

"You have a sharp memory."

"So do you."

"So are you so confused at the reasons for your interest in her?"

"Her name is Shaila."

"You still haven't answered my question about Shaila."

"I still don't feel the need."

"I am throwing a small party tonight in my house."

"Congrats."

"For what?"

"There must be some reason for the party in which I am least interested, but since you are interested in my wishes, I extend them to you."

"I want you to come."

"I told you I am not interested."

"I heard that but the party will not start without you. That's a promise and I always fulfil my promises."

"Nice habit."

"I know."

"Are we done here or do you need to tell me something else?"

"That's all for now, I guess."

"So, can I go back to work?"

"Here is my address. See you there," Sheena said, before leaving a piece of parchment on Vimarsh's table.

35

"My Ronnie got promoted yesterday," Anchit's mother said.

She had arrived from her small town to stay with her only son. Numerous so-called friends of Anchit were seated in a plush living room. Vimarsh and Shaila were also invited to this unassuming gathering. Anchit was still missing from the scene due to some urgent meeting.

"Promoted? Oh yes," Vimarsh said, as if woken up from a dream.

"Looking back on those years…skimping and starving…with my Ronnie as my only hope for a bright future. Well, I obviously never expected this day to arrive so soon," her face glowed with pride and satisfaction. Her stout body was leaning against the chair, in her properly creased cotton saree. "But who am I to judge how capable my Ronnie is when the whole world is watching his every move and recognising his talents?" she continued, more than happy to discuss her favourite subject with Vimarsh, Ramita, Shaila and many others. "Well, obviously being a mother, I would never have boasted about my Ronnie's qualities, but that's how it is. Some mothers are plain lucky while some aren't. I can only thank God for every small mercy. But if my Ronnie doesn't reach the grades of the elite within the next few summers, his mother would want to know the reason."

Shaila was looking more vexed with the scarcity of water in her body.

"Oh I forgot to ask…"

Shaila felt hopeful about her thirst being taken care of.

"…How much is your pay package?"

Ramita looked at Vimarsh for a split second, but he was looking straight at Anchit's Mom without skipping a beat.

"Mrs Saxena, can I have some water, please?" Shaila asked shamelessly.

"Hmm…yeah sure," she looked at Shaila as if unable to recognise her, but moved swiftly from her place.

"What the hell is she made up of?" Shaila whispered as Mrs Saxena disappeared.

"Anchit never wanted me to meet her. Now I know why," Ramita told Shaila, ignoring Vimarsh completely.

"Here," Mrs Saxena said, returning soon enough. "So where were we? Yes, you were telling me about your pay package."

"Aunty, it is not much; just around five," Ramita said with obvious irritation in her voice.

"Oh, that is sad. My poor child, how do you meet your expenses?"

"Aunty it is enough. I am happy," Ramita said, defending herself.

"Yes, what other option do we have other than to remain happy with our meagre means! Even though my Ronnie gives me his entire salary, I still find it difficult to run the house in that skimpy amount of two lakh every month. Son, what about you?" Now she turned to look hopefully at Vimarsh.

"What about *me*?" Vimarsh said effortlessly, laying stress on *me* at the end.

"I mean how are you doing?"

"I am doing alright, Mrs Saxena," Vimarsh said.

"That's good," Mrs Saxena conceded, though looking unsatisfied with his replies. "A guy like you should get at least fifty thousand per month. I mean look at you – you are smart and capable."

Vimarsh looked uncomfortable as all eyes were focused on him now.

"But still I want to know, is the company paying enough to all *my children*?" she said, emphasising the last two words.

"Mrs Saxena, they are paying me enough, which is one of the reasons I am continuing with them from so long. And you are right because even with the monthly salary of 2.3 lakh, I find it difficult to cover my expenses. I mean the two plots of land which I bought for forty lakh each and my other investments of around twenty lakhs are totally inadequate. There is so much more to do in life apart from these minor investments, isn't it?"

"Good, very good, son. Let me see if the maid has prepared something for you people to eat," Anchit's mother got up again to disappear behind the curtain, this time for a longer period.

Shaila giggled slowly as Ramita looked at Vimarsh from the corner of her eye. Everyone silently thanked him for saving them.

He opened the newspaper to avoid the attention.

SCORE: Vimarsh=2, Ramita=1.

ॐ

Vimarsh felt the coldest vibes when he entered his office that day. He looked sideways for the source.

"Hi Sheena, any problem?"

"None that you can solve."

"Thanks for the heads up," Vimarsh smiled.

ॐ

It was lunch time.

"What do you think of yourself?"

Vimarsh looked at the source of the voice. "Good to see you here. Come and have something."

"Why didn't you come?" Sheena asked, trying to keep her voice under control but still people were looking towards them.

"Sit, do not create a scene here," Vimarsh warned her.

Sheena looked at him with surprise but nevertheless obeyed without resistance.

"Hi Pratyush," Vimarsh said, looking behind her.

"Hi, Vimarsh!"

"Had your lunch?" Vimarsh said, shifting his glance from him to her.

"About to get it."

"Why don't you join me? I mean, us," Vimarsh smirked as Sheena's expression changed from bad to worse.

"Vimarsh…but…"

"Chill *yaar*, take your plate and come here."

"Okay," Pratyush left to get his food from the counter.

"Why did you call him?"

"He was in your team, right? You two must have a lot to catch up. I know the workload and clumsy schedules leave us with very little time to interact with our former teammates."

"Don't give me that shit. You know I don't like him."

"No, I don't know," Vimarsh said, acting brilliantly to appear visibly surprised.

"Don't tell me? I know you are aware of everything."

"So you mean those rumours are true?"

She glared at him with fiery eyes and walked out, stamping her feet in anger.

Everyone in the office knew that Sheena had started avoiding Pratyush since he started working directly under Vishvesh. Rumours were afloat that Sheena had no use for him since he couldn't assist her in any of her office work. She also got him thrown from her apartment when he tried to ask her the reason for avoiding him.

He had even toyed with the idea of chucking up his job but someone convinced him to stay and eventually took him in his team.

Part VI

Vimarsh

36

"Hi!" Sheena greeted Vimarsh as he was packing his bag. The office was already deserted.

"Hi!" Vimarsh looked at her for a fleeting moment.

It was Friday and Sheena was looking smokin' hot in a low-cut top and low waist jeans.

"It's too dark outside."

"It is 8:30, so it ought to be dark," Vimarsh moved towards the exit. "Want a lift?"

Sheena moved quickly towards her cubicle to get her bag.

"If you want to go by bus, I can drop you at the nearest bus stop." It was drizzling.

"I like rain," Sheena said.

Vimarsh kick started the bike.

"I love long drives, do you?" Her one hand was on his shoulder and the other on his thigh. She was leaning on his back.

"I wish I had a boyfriend and we could go on long drives at a moment's notice," her hand moved from his thigh towards his crock.

"Don't you talk while you drive?" she rubbed him slowly, whispering silently into his ears.

"You can take a bus from here," Vimarsh stopped at the bus stop.

She gave him an apprehensive look, but he showed no emotion.

She reluctantly obeyed.

"Have a great weekend."

"You too," she snapped. She waited for the bus when a bike halted at some distance from her, screeching to a halt.

"So you have come back."

"Sheena, one simple piece of advice. I don't know why you are like this, but I know that deep down you are very sensitive. Some events in one's life can change the whole course in a matter of seconds, though some things inside us never change. And I know you are still the same simple Sheena with whom I would like to form a lifelong friendship. Think about it. Till then, I can drop you till your house."

～◎～

"Hi!" Vimarsh said, rubbing his eyes.

"Hi…Vimarsh! This is Ramita."

"Can you hold for a sec?" Vimarsh covered the speakers, trying to curb his excitement. "Yes Ramita, tell me."

"Actually Vimarsh, Anchit had asked me to tell you that this weekend we are not going for bowling."

"No problem."

"I mean you can make some other plan."

"Yeah, now I have to. Let's see," Vimarsh said, giving a friendly snort.

"But at such short notice, what will you do?" Ramita lingered.

"I don't know. Let's see if Shaila has some plan in which I can join her."

"You can join us in case you don't find anyone else," Ramita said carelessly. The damage done was immense and it was too late to back-track. Still she decided to mend the fences, "I mean it is because of us that you are not going anywhere."

Vimarsh couldn't stop smiling. "Tell me the place and time. If nothing materialises, then I might come there."

"There is a famous café near UB city. You can join us there at 4 p.m. today?"

"I will give you a call around 1 o'clock if I happen to decide to reach there."

"That will be great," Ramita said nervously and hung up the phone.

～◎～

"Vimarsh…Vimarsh!"

"What's happened…Nick?"

"I am fuckin' going to die."

'Sorry this time it's my turn,' Vimarsh thought.

"No, you are not," Vimarsh said.

"Yes I am. Can't you fuckin' see?"

"What I am seeing is that you have not washed the clothes."

"Don't give me this fuckin' crap. Vimarsh…help me."

"I have to go somewhere."

"Your best friend is dying here and you are leaving him alone?"

"Okay, okay, I will stay behind," Vimarsh said, irritatingly.

The clock struck 11:30 and Vimarsh looked at it desperately. He wanted to call her but the strategy was to wait till 1:15.

The wait was unbearable.

"Vimarsh…where are you? I am hungry."

He ignored it.

"Vimarsh…Vimarsh."

"What?"

"Please don't shout. I am dying and hungry too."

༄༅༄

The phone rang.

"Pick up the phone…someone," Nick shouted in vain.

"Hello, Nick here," Nick coughed.

……………

"Oh hi, Mom…"

……………

"No, I am okay…no, seriously…no need for you to come here."

……………

"I was joking with him…I am not sick or anything."

……………

"Mooooooooooooom…no, no need to come here."

……………

"I am fine……yeah I will be a good boy."

……………

"But he started it."

....

"Why have I to apologise? It was just a joke."

....

"But I did it for the first time…Okay for the fourteenth time, but……"

....

"Okay, I will say sorry…also give him a treat…happy?"

....

"ALL RIGHT…'bye…yeah, yeah…'bye. Will call you in the evening…*haan,* I won't forget…'bye."

⁓ೞ⁓

"Vimarsh…Vimarsh," Nick knocked on the door.

"Yes…Nick."

"I just wanted to tell you that I am fine now and you can go wherever you want to."

"Thanks, Nick," Vimarsh smiled as he closed the door.

"Vimarsh," he knocked again.

Vimarsh opened the door.

"Well played."

"Thank you. Glad you appreciated it," Vimarsh replied.

"And Mom asked me to say sorry to you, so I am sorry."

"Apology accepted."

"Apology accepted…huh?" Nick mimicked as he closed the door.

⁓ೞ⁓

"Hi!" Vimarsh greeted Ramita.

"Hi!" she looked nervous.

"Where is everyone else?"

"What happened about your plans with Shaila?"

"I haven't talked to her yet."

"They will be a bit late."

"Oh, okay."

"What happened? You look disappointed," Ramita asked, looking anxious.

"Nothing of that sort...what do you want to have?"

"I will have beer."

"Okay."

"You don't look surprised like my other guy friends."

"You are not my friend...just an acquaintance."

"Why do you look at me like the way you do?"

"Because you want me to look at you in that way...beer for two please."

"I will have coffee."

"Okay one beer and one coffee."

"Make it two coffee and no beer please."

Vimarsh said nothing in return.

"They are not coming, right?"

"*No*," Ramita said emphatically in reply, her fretfulness gone. They sat in silence.

"This coffee is good," Vimarsh began.

"I don't think so."

"It is good that you don't."

"What is good? Tell me Vimarsh."

"Sitting here with me and that too without telling Anchit about it. This definitely doesn't come in the category of good."

"I hate your guts."

"And I love you."

She gave him the coldest of her stares and walked out of the café. Vimarsh kept on sipping his drink.

SCORE: Vimarsh=3, Ramita=2.

37

"Hello Anchit. This is Vimarsh."

"Vimarsh?"

"We met in the café…remember?"

"Café! Oh yes…yes…Sorry, I have a very bad memory. So what's up?"

"Hey, where are you guys these days? No contact or anything…I thought we could hang out sometime."

"Yeah, sure, sure! Why not? But not this week."

"Why, what's happened?"

"Ramita has gone to some silly place in Kerala with her friends."

"Silly place? Which silly place?"

"I think…porn…no, no…Ponmudi but she will come by this weekend. Then we can…"

"Hey, I have to go…'bye."

"Yeah okay, 'bye," but there was no one on the other side to accept that lonely 'bye.

The flight landed at Trivandrum International Airport. The airport was deserted barring a few yawning security personnel and it was raining, though both seemed unrelated.

"Ponmudi?…Will take at least two-and-a-half hours in this weather. Planning to stay there or only sightseeing and coming back at night?" the cab driver asked in his punctured English.

"How much?"

"Eight hundred bucks."

"I will give you sixteen hundred bucks if you will help me to find someone."

The cab driver looked at him with 'who-is-this-freak?' expression but the attraction of easy money prompted him to ignite the engine.

❦

It was almost noon when they reached Ponmudi.

"The best hotel...go there first."

Ponmudi was a relatively small town and it was almost unbelievable that it held such unexplored beauty in its heart. A sleeping bride, careless about her elegance and beauty. The splendour stretched itself on both sides of the road. Vimarsh sat spellbound, finding it almost impossible to find words to describe the grandeur, though he longed to drink every bit of its beauty.

They had already searched three hotels and were now inching closer to the fourth.

'There could be no better place for me to meet you,' Vimarsh thought.

"Stop...stop there. Near that florist," Vimarsh said, shocked to find Ramita at a roadside joint.

"Thanks man...here is your money," Vimarsh said, turning his wallet upside down at some distance from the joint.

"Thank you, sir," the cab driver said, still unable to believe his luck.

Vimarsh paid no heed. He was busy looking at his life who stood just a few metres away from him, completely oblivious of his presence. He didn't remember how long he kept on standing there, awestruck.

Ramita came out of the shop unaware and lost in her thoughts. All of a sudden, she found herself at a standstill, just a few feet away from him, astonished at finding a familiar face in a strange place.

He stared straight at her. She drew close to him.

"Hi!" he said.

"Hi!"

Vimarsh didn't know what to say next. "I thought you must be mad at me after that day, so I came to apologise," though unwarranted and unplanned, the dice was rolled. She looked at him with amazement.

"Oh!"

"I am sorry. I should not have expressed my feelings for you when I don't know you properly."

"It's okay. Hey wait! My friends are coming…I will introduce you to them as my old school friend."

✧◦✧

"So you have came 500 kilometres merely to apologise."

"That day I expressed myself in a hurry. I thought I owe you a better apology at least before you come to a conclusion about me."

"That day your gestures suggested that you hated me for being a brat."

"You made me travel all the way to be here just to see you. It freaks the hell out of me when I think that I couldn't live a day without seeing you and I really hate you for this."

"You know that Anchit and I are in a relationship or did I forget to tell you?"

"I never asked you to love me, but you can't stop me from loving you; you can't stop me from thinking about you and you can't stop me from looking at you the way I want to or did I miss something while expressing my feeling?"

Ramita remained quiet.

"I know, it is difficult for you…," Vimarsh paused. "Okay, let's forget this love, etc…Let's just be friends."

"Friends!" Ramita sounded confused.

"That will make your life easier, I guess."

She said nothing except to look at him intently, maybe to search for some sense of deceit or trick.

"Okay…let's be friends."

Vimarsh extended his hand. Ramita's met him midway.

"You know what? You are crazy."

"I know but when I see you, I think all this is worth it."

"Why?"

"When I saw you for the first time, you can't even imagine when it was, but I vividly remember that everything else around me just faded away. No one can ever be like you. Trust me."

Ramita blushed, turning away her gaze.

"No seriously, the searing pain was more than a heart attack but it was worth enduring…hey, now you are laughing? Tell me, has no one ever told you that you are the prettiest girl in this whole universe? Guys even go gaga over below-average-looking girls and here you are an epitome of beauty and no one has ever told you that?"

Ramita felt her cheeks redden and heart beat faster than usual. "May be no one has looked at me like the way you see me."

"Not even Anchit?" he asked.

She said nothing. He moved his eyes to the beautiful background with her in the middle. Nature has its own way of making splendid memories unforgettable.

"Good that you understood," he said, after a long pause.

"Tomorrow we are leaving by a tourist bus. You want to join us?"

"Okay."

"But don't forget that we have agreed to be only friends."

"Don't worry, I'll remember. Whatever I feel is within me…locked and you won't even feel it."

SCORE: Vimarsh=4, Ramita=50.

38

"Hey, where are you? The bus is about to leave."

"I am here, outside, talking to Garima."

"Garima…who?"

"Garima…your friend," Vimarsh replied.

Ramita disconnected the call.

It had been almost two hours and the bus was moving at full speed. Ramita felt irritated at the incessant laughter of Garima, cutting across from the last but one seat.

The bus stopped at a hotel. It was already half past midnight.

"You want something?" Garima asked, as she dashed out from the bus.

"No but hey…thanks for asking," Vimarsh smiled.

"No problem, sweetie."

Something inside Ramita flipped.

The bus was now deserted with almost everyone outside.

"Move," Ramita ordered.

"What?"

"Are you moving or not?"

"Do whatever you want, you whack-a-doodle! So you guys are shifting here or what? No problem…Garima and I will shift."

"Just shut up."

"Hey Ramita, you are on my seat," Garima said as soon as she returned. Vimarsh grinned, looking at his feet.

"Yeah, just chatting about our school days…you know. Can you sit there for some time?"

"Oh okay," Garima said, looking rather disappointed.

༺༒༻

"So, what joke were you telling her?"

"No jokes, only some real life stories."

"Ohh…cool."

They sat in silence. The lights inside the bus had been switched off as night descended into darkness.

"What about you and Shaila?"

"What about her?"

"What about you guys?"

"Just good friends," Vimarsh grinned in the darkness.

Ramita said nothing.

"Are you feeling cold?" he asked, looking at her movements.

"What do you think?"

"Wait," he got up and took out a blanket from his bag and wrapped her in a way that his hand was now in place of her headrest.

She said nothing. He expected nothing.

Vimarsh looked at her hand, which was resting on the common handrest.

He fondled it softly with his fingers. She looked at him. He kept on looking at her hand. She tried to move it away but he held it softly. Their eyes met for a split second. Finally she succeeded in getting her hand away from his grasp. He looked sideways and noticed everyone was fast asleep.

He looked at her and she at him. Their gaze met again, stayed a split second longer. She turned to look outside the window. The lone highway lay deserted. He stroked her hair with his fingers. She closed her eyes. He removed a few strands from her face. Her heart began to beat loudly. She looked at him again with pleading eyes, *'What are you doing to me?'*

'Treasuring this night forever in my memory,' he reflected back.

She leaned towards him, still looking out. He kissed her behind her ears. Her breathing got heavy and she turned her face as her kohl-filled eyes hugged him with longing. She rested her head on his shoulders.

He raised her face to look at her more closely. She closed her eyes. He kissed her on the cheeks, but she instinctively pushed him back. He turned his face away from her.

Nothing had changed in the last few minutes in that bus which was lolling on the sleepy road. But for two of its occupants, the world had turned upside down.

He again looked at her as she was scratching her nails, while looking outside. The tension was unbearable for him. He felt like choking. He wanted to breathe and soon. His end seemed near. He looked at her but she was still looking outside, completely oblivious about his plight. He turned her face towards him but she showed no emotions. She felt his soft lips on hers and the two closed their eyes before slipping into the ecstasy of their lives.

And then a resounding slap drove them apart.

"What happened?" someone asked, waking up.

"These mosquitoes, I tell you," Ramita said in a hurry.

"Oh…okay," and the voice again drowned into sleep.

An unruly stillness spread itself again.

"Sorry," Vimarsh said, looking at her.

"I am sorry," Ramita replied.

"No it was my mistake."

SCORE: Vimarsh=-50, Ramita=100.

39

"Hi, can I talk to Vimarsh?"

"Who is it?"

"This is Anchit."

"Oh…Anchit, how are you?"

"Hey, I was thinking that we all can meet this weekend. Ramita has also arrived from Kerala."

'So she has not told him anything, yet.' "Okay."

"There is a new international lounge bar on MG Road. We can go there."

"That will be great. See you there," Vimarsh hung up the phone.

"So, what do you want to have?" Vimarsh asked Shaila.

Ramita looked at Vimarsh with disgust.

"Sweety, what should I order?" Ramita caressed Anchit's arm, looking at Shaila from the corner of her eye.

"Whatever you wish for, darling," Anchit reciprocated with the same love in his tone.

"Sir, can I have your order please?" the barman asked with utmost sincerity.

"One large whisky on the rocks, one beer for the gentleman and red wine for the ladies," Anchit ordered, taking the liberty of giving the instructions on everyone's behalf. "Is that okay, Vimarsh?"

"I guess so," Vimarsh looked carefully at the barman. He waited for a split second before imparting his instructions. "A dry martini…," he said. "…One in a champagne glass."

"Yes sir," the barman replied promptly.

"Just a second please…yeah, add three measures of vodka, one-third of vermouth, half measure of Smirnoff citrus twist vodka. Shake until it is ice cold and add this in the end. Got it?" Vimarsh completed his requirements while showing the last part of the drink in a piece of paper.

"Certainly sir," the barman said, looking surprisingly pleased.

"And for the lady…," Vimarsh looked at Shaila, "would you like if I order something other than red wine for you?"

"I would love to try it," Shaila beamed at him.

"Add the champagne to the flute last. Add one measure of gin, half measure of lemon juice and a little bit of sugar and stir it gently afterwards and one-third measure of the same in the end. Am I sounding reasonable enough?"

"Certainly sir," and he left.

"How did you know all this?" Ramita asked.

"What?" Vimarsh asked innocently.

"You know what I am talking about," Ramita replied, revealing her mock anger.

"The secret is something which I can't reveal, but thanks for giving me these shocking praiseworthy expressions."

"Excuse me sir," a middle-aged, partly bald man, interrupted their good old ways, "sorry for interrupting you."

"Not a problem. Tell me," Anchit replied.

"May I know the gentleman who ordered these two drinks?" he asked, looking curious.

"Yeah, it's me," Vimarsh said.

"Hello sir, I am the manager in charge here. May I have a word with you, in my cabin please?" he asked politely.

"Is there anything serious?" Anchit asked, trying to look worried but failing to do so.

"No sir, not at all. There is nothing to be worried about."

Vimarsh followed him to his cabin.

"Why did the manager himself call him?" Shaila looked agonised.

"I don't know. We have been here many times but nothing like this has ever happened. Right Anchit?"

"May be the drinks he had ordered are not acceptable to the authorities," Anchit said, trying to sound convincing.

He was truly enjoying all the attention and questions that were thrown at him by the two ladies. But the glee lasted only for twenty-two minutes, because Vimarsh, accompanied by the manager and a gentleman in quite an expensive Versace suit, returned, walking towards their group.

"Thank you, Vimarsh. We will get back to you at the earliest," said the new entrant, shaking hands with Vimarsh. "Hi guys! We have good news for you. Today your drinks are on the house...bon appétit. Mr Khurana, please take good care of them," he instructed the manager.

"Definitely sir, it would be a pleasure."

"Okay guys, enjoy your drinks," he said and left with a broad smile.

"Thanks Jake," Vimarsh shook his hand.

"Hey what happened? Who was he?" Ramita asked curiously, as the wait had finally got on her nerves.

"Vimarsh, don't say that he offered you a million for your weird cocktail of drinks," Anchit added sarcastically.

"Hey, how do you know? Actually he offered me not one but ten million for the recipe that I had ordered for Shaila and also 2.5 per cent as royalty from the sales over lifetime. He is the country head of this lounge chain. He and his wife were in the office when the barman to whom we had given the order brought that recipe to his notice and his wife, who herself happens to be a connoisseur. She tasted it herself and liked it. According to her, she had never tasted anything like that in her whole life. They are sending it to their drink-makers for further tests and on receiving a report from there, they will legally buy the recipe. The whole thing will take around twenty days. They asked me to consult my lawyers once I receive the agreement."

"Are you kidding?" Shaila asked ecstatically.

"Hey, this is not the kind of joke I like," Ramita said.

"It is a reality. And you know, what will be the name of the drink?"

"Don't tell me. It is on your name."

"Well, you are again right but partly. The name I had given to it was Shaila. It will be called on your name," Vimarsh said, looking fondly at Shaila.

Shaila sat dumbstruck, not knowing what to say. Her eyes were almost moist when Vimarsh held her hand softly.

"I know," Vimarsh said softly.

"But you should have given it your name," Ramita said, miffed all the unwanted attention Shaila was getting.

"I thought of it for the first six minutes after he asked me about the name, but then I remembered that Shaila's friendship day's gift was pending with me."

"I love you," Shaila kissed Vimarsh. "This is the best gift of my whole life."

Ramita was almost red with rage but moreover, why was she giving so much importance to Vimarsh when Anchit was better than him in everything?

Anchit was equally miffed at the sudden turn of events. Despite all his efforts, he had been unable to beat the dumb and ugly Vimarsh.

Vimarsh's mobile flashed brightly to show an incoming text.

"Accepted."

Vimarsh smiled.

"Welcome aboard," he wrote.

The delivery message confirmed that the message had been rightly delivered to its intended recipient…*Sheena*.

The evening never looked so bright to Vimarsh. He remembered Chris for having faith in him when nobody did; not even him.

SCORE: Vimarsh=100, Ramita=100.

40

"What's happened? Why did you call me here?"

Ramita said nothing. The small café was deserted with a few customers parking or getting ready to leave.

Vimarsh sat down. "I don't know…what's the matter with you? In Ponmudi, you said we will be friends then…do friends behave like this? How dare you hold my hand? If Anchit would have known this…"

"I also kissed you after that? Didn't you notice that? Why didn't you stop me after the first time? And why did you come to see me at the lounge bar when you have problems with all this?" Vimarsh said sarcastically.

Ramita chose to adopt silence. The rising tension was dreadful for him but he said nothing.

"Isn't this love…? I kissed you there because I saw love in your eyes. I know you want me…you are sitting there and I am here but I want to sit with you, holding you in my hands and I know you want the same."

Ramita looked at him with angry eyes.

"I asked you to be friends because I thought we could be one, but in the bus everything got shattered. The scent of your hair drove me insane. I felt I was about to die if I were not to kiss you there."

"I don't know what you are talking about."

'Why are you such a riddle, Ramita?'

"Ramita, you are practical and sensible but don't say 'no'. You like me I know…It happens once in a lifetime and if we can't live with the person we love, then what is the use of living? Look at me…" he paused. "You know what, this is fuckin' unbelievable."

"One more time if you say that word you will see me leave."

"You know what? You can keep on acting but one day Anchit will know that you don't love him. Then, what will you do? Keep on living in denial and make him suffer or leave him to die with sorrow?"

"It doesn't matter any more. Anchit and I are getting engaged. His Mom and my parents have fixed the date for two weeks ahead. They were already planning about it from a long time."

"Did you know about it when we were in the bus?"

"No, Anchit told me about this after we left the lounge. My parents confirmed it today. The wedding is next month."

He said nothing. There was nothing left for him to say.

"What do you want me to do now, Vimarsh?"

"Go and get engaged. Get married, have kids of someone you don't love. You didn't come here to take my permission. You just wanted to inform me and you have done. I have heard it…now get lost."

She looked at him with utmost disgust.

"By the way…congrats for the engagement. I won't be here at that time. So convey these to your would-be too."

"Where are you going?"

"None of your concern…Shaila and I are going somewhere."

"Thanks for your wishes," Ramita said acerbically.

I hate you. I really do. Why are you doing this to me and yourself,' he thought.

SCORE: Vimarsh=100, Ramita=200.

41

"Hello…Vimarsh," a sweet voice greeted him.

"Oh…hi Ramita!" It had been two days since he had heard her soothing voice. The last time they had met, Ramita had left in anger but now she seemed normal. Why?

"Listen, Anchit is throwing a party for our engagement this Saturday and you have to come," Ramita said, speaking in a hurry. And now he knew why!

"This Saturday…oh…sorry Ramita, this Saturday I have other plans, so can't come. But anyway, you guys enjoy," Vimarsh said, feeling guilty for smiling.

"*Yenti* (what) plans Vimarsh? No plans. You have to…have to… have to come."

"Ramita, try to understand. Shaila and I are already going out for dinner that night and I have promised her that I will be a good boy all day and help her in shopping for the trip," Vimarsh said, winking at Shaila who glared at him with shock.

Ramita felt a surge of jealousy on hearing the name.

"I don't know anything; the party is at the Anchit's friend's farm-house. The address I am texting you. I will meet you there, otherwise never talk to me again."

"Cute…" Vimarsh laughed. "I can't promise anything but for Anchit's sake, I will try. Okay, I have to go…talk to you later…'bye."

"But Vimarsh…," Ramita wanted to say so much more but the call was over.

Ramita could not concentrate on her work.

'What is it with this Shaila? Why does Vimarsh gives her so much value? And why am I bothered about whom Vimarsh goes to dine with?

No, no I should concentrate on Anchit. He loves me…I love him…we are getting engaged…Vimarsh is just a friend…JUST A FRIEND WHOM I HATE,' thought Ramita. But her mind was beyond her control. It hovered again and again over Shaila and Vimarsh. Her fingers kept playing with the keys of her mobile phone.

'Should I call him again and ask him to change his plans? No, I should not call him. What will he think of me? The party will be more rocking even if he and his Shaila are not there.'

"Hello Anchit."

"What's happened, Ramita? I am in the midst of a meeting. Why are you calling me again and again? Can't you understand that when someone rejects your call, it means he is busy. Okay, tell me, what is it?"

"Nothing…okay 'bye."

"You called me for saying nothing. Okay c'mon, tell me, what has happened?" Anchit said, softening his voice without success.

"Leave it. You concentrate on your meeting."

"No, now I am outside the meeting room. C'mon, tell me."

"Can we give the party on some other weekend?"

"Why the hell do you want that now? You yourself agreed to these dates and now…when everything is arranged, then…"

"Now I want them to be changed. Is there any problem in that?"

"Ramita, we will talk about it after this meeting is over. Now I have to go. Okay 'bye," and another dialer tone greeted Ramita.

42

"What has happened to your dinner?" Ramita asked sardonically, looking at Vimarsh.

"Nothing, it is still on. Actually Shaila and I have decided to have our dinner here itself. You know the place does not matter; it's the feelings that count."

"Hi Shaila," Ramita forcibly uttered these two words. "But this is not the place where one can hold mushy romantic dinner dates," she said to Vimarsh.

"I know but after you failed to postpone the party to some other day, I thought it advisable not to break your heart, so we have come," Vimarsh said, looking at the shining water in the pool.

Ramita felt as if she stood naked and someone had turned all the lights on her. "How do you know…?"

"It doesn't matter how I know or what I know. The main thing is that this party desperately needs some life," Vimarsh said, looking at the girl seated at the poolside. "Excuse me ladies."

"Rascal…," Ramita said looking at Vimarsh's back.

"He is cute," Shaila interrupted.

"How long have you known him?"

"Not much, but one thing I know is that the girl whom he marries will be very lucky. I just wish that…anyways, let's enjoy the party."

"HEY, WHAT HAPPENED TO THE LIGHTS?"

"Wait, I will go and check," Anchit said, trying to figure out his way in the mobile light.

"I think there is a power cut in the whole area. It seems that it has gone for a long time. Is there any generator or inverter?" Vimarsh asked. His eyes were fixed on Ramita who was looking magnificent in the moonlight.

"No nothing, both the inverters have gone for repair," Anchit's friend, owner of the farmhouse, said with disappointment.

"Okay, so you have any cave-men light-producing equipment, like candles or torches?"

"May be, I am not sure. I have to look."

"Hey, it's so hot here. We are going back home," a few voices muttered in the dark.

Vimarsh could still see Ramita's eyes which were about to flood with tears.

"You are right; it is hot in here…so what should we do?"

"Hey, I have got some candles."

"Guys, this is a signal from gawd," Vimarsh said, standing up on a chair. His face shone in the light of the candles.

"What signal?" someone exclaimed.

Anchit looked apprehensive about this new drama.

"That we do not need this boring party. Actually…guys, we need a pool party," and saying that, he jumped into the pool, splashing water all around.

"Wow!" said someone and with that some more bodies jumped into the pool followed by some more. One of the guys took out his guitar and a new kind of a party started.

MOONLIGHT POOL BASH.

It was 2 in the night when the electricity finally returned, but by then everybody was drenched in water and sweat.

"Hey Vimarsh, that was really rocking. Thanks dude. Anyway, I am Ayesha. I am throwing a party next weekend at my house. Why don't you join us there?"

"For beautiful girls, I am always game. See you at the party," Vimarsh said.

"This is my number. Give me a call sometime," Ayesha said with a playful smile. Vimarsh looked at the number for two seconds and then at the girl again.

"Sure. Okay, I have to go now. Nice meeting you and thanks for this," he said, waving the number at her.

"Bye."

"Who was she?" Ramita asked.

"No idea, met her for the first time," Vimarsh lied, looking straight into Ramita's eyes.

"What was she saying? Is this her number?"

"She was inviting me to her party next weekend."

"And what did you say?"

"You know I can't say 'no' to anyone."

"Oh really!"

"Hey, what are you doing?" Vimarsh asked, trying to stop Ramita from tearing the piece of paper, which a few moments ago had contained a ten-digit number.

"Next week, you are taking me out for shopping."

"Shopping for what? Your engagement ceremony? You want me to help you in shopping for your engagement? Are you kidding?" Vimarsh laughed like hell. "Hell, I don't want to be a *kabab mai haddi* between you and Anchit," Vimarsh threw back.

"YOU means you and me. By the way, he is going on a tour this Tuesday for ten days and I am not going to take any excuses this time…no office, no dinner and no Shaila, nothing. Okay? And just keep quiet about this. Okay?"

"Are you planning to have an extra engagement affair with me?"

"Shut up."

Vimarsh felt it was better to stay quiet.

"And…thanks for today. It was the best night of my life," Ramita smiled and left.

"Second best night."

"Shut up," Ramita hissed, looking embarrassed.

SCORE: Vimarsh=300, Ramita=200.

☙୨◊୧❧

"You love her too much," Shaila said, looking at Vimarsh.

"I don't have any other option."

"Then why don't you tell her?"

"No it is better this way. She will understand one day," Vimarsh said. He did not want to tell anyone about his Ponmudi trip.

"But she is getting engaged."

"But for a few days she is still single."

"I don't understand you."

"Don't worry, one day you too will understand," Vimarsh sighed.

43

'What next?' he wondered while getting ready to shop for the engagement ceremony of his heartthrob.

"Hi! Looking good in stripes."

"Why did you ask me to come here? We were going for shopping, right?" There was no need for exchange of greetings.

"No…we are not. Anchit's tour has been cancelled. I called you here since I didn't want to be seen with you near our office. Shall we go?"

"Where?"

"Wherever. We have four hours."

"Forum, Koremangala."

She nodded her head in affirmation.

"We can watch some movie till half time and then go out for dinner," she suggested.

❧

"You know Anchit is very possessive about me. He does not let me go anywhere alone. As for the trip to Ponmudi, he was mad at me for agreeing to go without consulting him. He didn't even talk to me for three weeks and didn't even visit me there. Today when I thought of meeting you for I wanted to spend some time with you and talk to you alone, I told him that I had some work which would take a large part of the evening. See, for this also I had to lie."

"WHAT?" It was more of a shock than a question.

"I lied."

Vimarsh smirked in the darkness of the theatre.

"Can you hear me?" Ramita asked hesitantly.

"Yes…go on."

"Vimarsh, let's just be friends, otherwise there will be too much pain…too much pressure. I don't want that. I feel like spending time with you…talking to you…and that is why I am here. Love will destroy it, I mean this thing between us."

☙❧

"One lime juice and one coffee."

"Can I tell this to Anchit when we meet tomorrow – that you and I are just friends without feeling guilty? If we don't have anything between us, you know we all can hang out together. What do you say?"

He still had nothing to say.

☙❧

The breeze ruffled Ramita's hair. It was almost 10 at night when they left the restaurant.

"Kiss…!"

"What about it?"

"Your girl would be very lucky."

"Why?"

☙❧

"Okay I will walk from here. I don't want my roommate to see me with you," Ramita said, getting off from the bike near a turn from her flat.

"What are you trying to prove, Ramita? That it is not a big deal? You talk about the kiss but you don't touch me when you are on the bike. You think that if your hands touched me I would…When we were in that bus, I wanted to kiss you. I felt like choking to death without kissing you. Even now, when you are a hundred feet away, still I feel like hugging you, caressing your hair, feeling your body in my arms. And I will feel the same even when I am ninety-years old…I WAN'NA MAKE LOVE TO YOU ALL THE TIME. THEN HOW CAN WE BE FRIENDS? Are you understanding me or not? You feel spending time with me is only because of love. Take it away and nothing will be there. You will feel nothing. You want to assure Anchit that we are mere friends. I am telling you this which I have not told anyone ever in life, from the moment I saw you, not a moment has passed when I have not thought of you. I have always imagined myself to be with you and now today, when, I am with you, I should be happy but I am not. I am in agony and the closer I get to you, the worse it gets. The very thought of not being with you makes my breath come to a grinding halt. I am haunted by the kiss that you should never have given to me. My heart beats rapidly and makes that kiss a scar with every passing moment. You are in my very soul, tormenting me. What can I do? I'll do anything you ask but not this."

"I HATE YOU."

"THANK YOU."

When she didn't like anything she walked away. He saw the back of her head more than her big black eyes. Nor that he was complaining.

'Why are you so difficult?' he wondered.

SCORE: Vimarsh=300, Ramita=500.

∼✧∽

"Pick up the phone, you idiot."

Vimarsh looked at the name flashing on his cell but chose to ignore it.

"Why are you not picking it up? It's Ramita, *naa*?" Shaila asked, looking at him quizzically.

"Today is her engagement with Anchit."

"What? Then what are you doing here in Tirupati with me? You should have been there," she paused for a moment. "You knew this all the time and yet you didn't tell me."

"You won't understand. I love her but I can't give her what she wants and deserves."

"What are you saying?"

"May be not today but some day you will understand. But it is true that I can't marry her without jeopardising her life. She is better off with Anchit. He can give her everything," Vimarsh said serenely, looking at the endless line of devotees standing in the narrow corridor of the shrine. He had stopped believing in God the day he had discovered about his abrupt end. But Shaila wanted to come here with him only and so he was here. Standing in the sea of tonsured heads, he was wondering about the existence of God.

'Why do we do these things to please him? What makes him tick among us mortals? Why do we want to believe in the belief that he is the ultimate answer to every damn setback?' Vimarsh struggled to find the answers to his numerous such questions, but failed. He glanced at Shaila who was standing in front of him in the queue, looking calmly at the proceedings.

After a long wait of six hours, the moment came for them to enter the main temple. The door looked as if stretching itself to accommodate the thousands of devotees in one go. Once they entered the small hall, they didn't have to walk a single step. They just flowed in the sea of people and Vimarsh found himself standing in front of a statue, some 100 feet away in a dark dungeon-like alley. He felt the eyes shine at him and for the first time he felt no fear in his life. A strange power flowed from the shrine into his body and through the eyes.

'I am still alive. I am not dead.'

The clock struck 12 but Ramita was still rolling on the bed in search of sleep. Her mind still hovered around Vimarsh. Something in him was making her want him so much. Never in her life had any man enticed her so much through his love and charm.

"Tch…Tch!"

"Vimarsh…!" she almost jumped from the bed.

"You are looking beautiful in this night suit."

"You are crazy. I was just thinking about you and you are here, IDIOT, what the hell are you doing in my balcony? Go," she whispered.

"I want to talk to you."

"No…I can't…go…hey…okay wait. I am coming. I have promised my parents that I won't see that stupid guy who is the sole reason of this drama again."

"His name is Vimarsh. You didn't tell them about me, did you?…I still want to know, why did you break your engagement? Is there some problem between you two because of me?" They were outside.

"I love you Vimarsh," she said, looking sideways.

"You realised this at your engagement?"

A smile passed between them.

"I have been in love with you since the moment I laid my eyes on you in the bus. First time was when I saw you in the café with Shaila. I wanted to cuddle you tightly. Your eyes are very naughty, do you know? The way you look at me always stirs me from inside…when in the cafe, you said that you loved me, I turned angry…I thought you had found out…but when you came to Ponmudi just to apologise to me, I fell in love with you again. I knew that it was love that's why I let you kiss me in the bus…which I had never even allowed to Anchit also. It was the best journey of my life. Happy now?" she said, smiling with a glint of naughtiness in her large deer-like eyes.

"You have never allowed Anchit to kiss you?"

"From all of that you could gather only this much? All guys are sick."

"No, I mean…"

"Shut up and come here," she said, snuggling close to him.

"Hey, what else did you tell Anchit?"

"About what?"

"About breaking off the engagement."

"Nothing."

"Nothing?"

"I mean I told him I was not ready yet."

"He did not suspect that you could be in love with someone else?"

"IIMs do not teach girl psychology…Now shut up."

"I love you."

"You are an idiot."

"You are awesome."

She beamed, closing her eyes.
SCORE: Vimarsh=1000, Ramita=1001.
The Game Begins Now.

45

"Hi Ramita!"

"Hi Anchit!"

An awkward silence followed.

"I…actually I need to talk to you," he said, looking sideways, whispering in an office full of robots working in front of computers. "Can we go to the meeting room?"

"Yeah, sure."

Anchit closed the door carefully and slowly as Ramita entered the room that was small but cosy, not to forget the formal interiors like an execution chamber.

"Hi…again," he said. The silence was hard to bear.

"Hi!" Ramita was still looking sideways.

"How are you doing?"

"Fine."

"Great…that is great," Anchit said and looked at the ceiling as if trying to read something.

"Anchit…whatever happened at the engagement ceremony…"

"I know…I put a lot of pressure on you."

"No, that's not…"

"I know…I know, you don't like Mom. If you want, we can shift to another place after marriage."

"Anchit…listen, I don't want you to leave your mother for me."

"If you are worried about what she will think about you, then don't. It will be my decision. I will convince her…make her understand."

"Anchit, you are not getting the point. I really need some space right now and also some more time to think about many things in life. And I think you too need the same." So saying, she began to walk out of the room.

"Is there someone else in your life?"

She stopped at the door, looked at him with amusement but said nothing. She closed the door…softly.

∽◉∾

She had taken only three or four steps.

"Ramita, it is going to rain. We must find shelter."

'Was she glad to see him?' "Vimarsh!" Instinctively, he moved forward and kissed her lightly on her forehead.

"Did I say you could?"

"I could what?"

"Did I say you could kiss me?"

"Sorry, but you are looking so stunning. I got carried away."

"But I didn't."

She didn't feel any remorse. It felt as the most natural gesture on her part.

They were walking alone. Though she had a car, he insisted on walking. The road was deserted. The drizzling continued.

"Have you ever been kissed by anyone in the rain?"

She looked at him, puzzled.

He kissed her but not on the forehead, and not lightly. It lasted a good, long time. She held on to the pockets of his half jacket during the long kiss…even after it was long done. Her hands were half inside the pockets, half hanging loose outside. Her eyes were closed. This was supposedly the best kiss of her life.

"I don't like it," Ramita said.

"Like what?" Vimarsh smiled.

"The fact that I like it."

They kept on walking and she kept on holding on to his pocket.

"Where are we?"

"You tell."

He didn't kiss her again to say goodbye and she didn't insist.

"I will not be able to call you for one or two months."

She said nothing for a few moments, only a few moments. "Why?" she asked after a small pause with deep furrows on her forehead.

"Because I will give you a call only when I reach my room," he said, turning his back towards her.

"RASCAL."

He didn't look back. He knew she was still looking at him, waiting for him to turn around, but he didn't.

Ramita waited for his phone but it did not buzz. She dialled his number.

"How can you be such a good kisser? How could anyone ever be?"

"I am a natural."

"I think I love you."

"I would take it as a friend's devotion."

"Do friends kiss like we did?" Ramita asked, neither unhappy nor surprised.

"Will tell you once we kiss again…goodnight."

❦

He felt an acute pain on the left side of his abdomen.

"Nick…NICK…NICKKKKKK!"

"WHAT? What happened?" Nick shouted. He was half-naked or half-dressed.

"My stomach…it's paining. I can't breathe."

"Did you take your medicine?"

"It's in the drawer."

"Okay," Nick said, moving fast for the first time in his life. He magically appeared with the pills in a matter of milliseconds.

Vimarsh swallowed them at lightning speed.

"Water," Nick said. "This is the third time this week."

"I know."

"You need to tell her."

"I will when it is time."

"You do not understand."

"No, you do not understand."

꧁꧂

"Why don't you come inside?" Ramita said to him that day.

"What about your roomies?"

"What about them?"

"Nothing," he said.

"What?"

"Nothing."

"Tell me," she insisted, tugging at his collar.

"You are always so concerned that your roomies might see us together."

"They are not here tonight."

He smiled.

"What is there to smile about?"

He entered the house. She didn't press for a reply.

"This is my room. Do you want anything?"

"I am hungry," he said and opened one of the cupboards of her room.

"Okay."

"Hey, who wears this?" he picked up one of her inner wears.

"Shut up," she snatched it from him in mock anger.

"Black will definitely suit you more."

"After marriage, buy whatever you want but don't suggest that crap now."

He smiled and opened her laptop which lay on the bed.

She left for the kitchen.

"When are your roommates coming?"

"Day after tomorrow. Why?"

"Nothing."

"Hey, come here and help me."

He went and sat on the slab in the kitchen.

"Don't just sit there. Chop these things."

He obeyed.

"What is it?" she asked when she caught him looking at her for the umpteenth time.

"Just imagining something."

"What?"

"You in black."

"If one more time you smile like this, I will kill you with this," she said, pointing the knife at his heart.

He laughed and kept on chopping.

"What? Stop looking at me like that."

"Why?"

"It makes me nervous."

"Okay," he said and began to look at his plate.

"Why do you agree with my every command?"

"Do I?"

"Yes, you do."

"Oh, I am sorry."

"You don't even let me play the entire game. You quit too soon."

"Why do you want to play games?"

"Don't know. Instinctive, I guess," she replied.

He looked at his plate again.

"You don't want to say anything," she said, breaking the silence.

"About what?"

"About me...of course."

"Why do you think I need to say something?"

"I don't know."

He said nothing for a while, but kept on grinning.

"Why do you smile so much?"

"Why do you care so much?"

"About what?"

"That one must play games in a relationship. You are beautiful and I am in love with you. That is the only truth here. I can never ever love anyone else."

"How can you be so blunt?"

"I am not. I am only telling you the facts of life and not my feelings which are only opinions. And opinions are prone to changes; facts aren't."

She looked at him with affection.

❧

"What should I wear?" he asked innocently.

She didn't question his assumption to stay overnight. He stretched his body on her small, cosy bed and opened her laptop again. She sat down on a corner of the bed, looking at him.

"If you want to change, then you can use some other room," he said.

She kept on looking at him as he diverted his gaze towards her laptop.

"Your phone is ringing."

"What?"

"Your phone…it's ringing."

"Oh…sorry."

She looked at it and silenced it.

"Is it Anchit?" he asked.

"No…I mean 'yes'. He calls me almost every half hour or something."

"Not today though…I think this is his first call today."

"I don't know."

"He still doesn't know about me?"

"No, he still doesn't know about *us*."

He smiled again.

"You know we are alone here."

"I know," he said, without looking at her.

The silence was soothing. She felt so much at peace with him that she kept on glancing at him again and again. He sat there on her bed – so close to her yet so far.

She couldn't control him like she controlled Anchit. Anchit was always concerned about her mood swings and demands, irrespective of their relevance or validity. But then, Anchit always cared about what others thought about him and his image. She felt like a trophy girlfriend with him. Even his smile was controlled by his bosses. She always felt that it was his vulnerability towards his responsibilities that made him do things which others would abhor or hate to perform. During the last days of their relationship, she had concluded that this was the only way he knew in life. Anchit always sought and treated others' advice as of prime importance rather than his own desires or thoughts. Ramita hated it but everyone in her vicinity behaved like Anchit when it came to their profession, even she herself but Vimarsh was unusual.

She couldn't help comparing Anchit with Vimarsh. Though she knew it was futile.

"Can you stop that please?" Vimarsh said, interrupting her train of thoughts.

"What?"

"It was just a phone call."

She looked at him sheepishly.

"Can you stop peeping into my private stuff?"

"I am not playing with any of your funny costumes. This is only your laptop," Vimarsh replied.

"We are alone here."

"I know that."

"This is my room and *this is my bed*. Get up from it," she ordered.

He came close to her. This was the weirdest moment of her life. She wanted him to hug her but all he was doing was to tease and elude her.

She kissed him. He didn't resist.

"What do you want? You are driving me nuts."

"What do I want? What I want is standing right here…in front of me. You still compare me with someone else. When will you stop doing that and start loving me for what I am? Then only will we cross the line. Till then we can stay like this."

She smiled. He knew her so perfectly that it really scared her. Was she becoming much too dependent on him? She didn't know. She didn't care.

"Good morning," he said.

She had slept on him the entire night. He was staring at her face when she opened her eyes. She kissed him again and for a much longer time.

"I don't want to go to office."

"Then don't go," he smiled.

And she closed her eyes again.

46

"Where are you?"

"I am in the Forum."

"What are you doing there?"

"Nothing."

"Get me something?" Ramita demanded.

"What?"

"I don't know…surprise me."

"Will try; can't promise. So don't expect much," he said and disconnected the call.

He felt a severe pain in his stomach. He rolled down on the pavement of the Mall. Everything before him went dark.

Vimarsh opened his eyes slowly.

"Shiva, what happened to him?" Nick was asking.

"We gave him an injection as soon as he was brought here."

"How much time…?"

"I don't know…the last option is operation, but we will wait till…"

Vimarsh closed his eyes slowly before slipping into darkness again.

※◎※

It had been almost three days since he was in the hospital. He had sent one message to Shaila to say that due to some urgent work he was leaving for his home town and another one to Ramita to announce that he was getting married to some girl in his hometown, as per his mother's wishes. That were the last acts of his before dumping his cell in the bottom shelf of his ward.

'It will be best for her,' he had thought.

※◎※

He opened his eyes.

Nick sat beside him. He felt naked inside the hospital robes but chose to ignore his discomfiture.

"How much time do I have?" he asked weakly.

"Fifteen more minutes."

"What…only fifteen minutes?"

"Why are you screaming?" Nick said.

"What should I do now?" Vimarsh felt the farce of not being able to see Ramita ever…or Shaila…or even Vishvesh…and Lingasamy. "I am dying here."

"NO ONE IS DYING HERE…YOU FUCK FACE," said Nick.

Vimarsh looked at him with incredulity.

※◎※

"Vimarsh?"

"Last name please."

She tried to remember.

"Kant Chaturvedi…Vimarsh Kant Chaturvedi."

"Room 157."

She ran and she ran damn hard. "Vimarsh…Vimarsh," she almost bellowed on seeing him on the bed. "Vimarsh…Vimarsh."

Nothing else moved in the room except for a few heels which clicked on the floor for the next few moments.

She sat on the bedside as tears welled up in her eyes.

"Why didn't you tell me about it?"

"I never got a chance."

"What has happened to your voice?"

"Damaged due to…"

"Oh Vimarsh, why did this happen to you of all the people?" Shaila asked, placing her head on the bed in despair.

He put his hand on her head to comfort her.

"WHO ARE YOU?" Shaila almost screeched.

"Don't shout…I am Nick."

"Where is Vimarsh and why did you keep that sheet on your face all this time?"

"Long story…if only you could sit down please."

❧◎❧

"What are you doing?" Vimarsh's voice echoed in the hall.

"What is he doing here at my son's wedding?" she bellowed.

"Who is he?" whispers floated in the hall. "What is he wearing… hospital robes and jeans?" some more whispered.

"What are you doing here?" Ramita looked shocked.

"You are getting married…why didn't you tell me?" Vimarsh asked.

"Why the hell were you not picking up your phone?"

"I was……"

"I know…you lied to me…you got married to Shaila."

"WHO TOLD YOU THIS CRAP?"

"THAT'S NONE OF YOUR BUSINESS," Ramita yelled back.

"IT WAS HIM…YOU CHOSE HIM OVER ME?" it was Anchit's turn to shout.

"I TOLD YOU…HE WILL BACKSTAB YOU ONE DAY," Anchit's Mom was now swinging her bat for her son.

Vimarsh ignored everyone. He kept on moving towards Ramita.

"I was in the hospital."

"What happened to you…AIDS? And what about that message about your hometown and your mother's last wish?" Ramita asked sarcastically.

"My parents died long ago in a car accident."

"You are such a loser, Vimarsh," Anchit spoke out.

"Trust me," Vimarsh said.

"FUCK YOU," Ramita bellowed. Anchit's Mom gasped at the words.

"SHUT UP."

"You keep on cheating on me and still think that I would remain an *abla naari*."

"Shut up…YOU BITCH," Vimarsh shouted, standing on the dais in his hospital robes and blue jeans.

It was a unique sight with the bride and groom standing with a patient on the stage.

"Why should I? Leave me…leave me…" Ramita screamed. Anchit tried to help her as all the guests were now out of breath as was Anchit's Mom too.

Anchit tried to get hold of Ramita from behind but Vimarsh held her tightly.

"Ramita, don't worry, I am calling the police," Anchit said.

Someone rapped on Anchit's knuckles and his mobile dropped on the floor.

"Ramita…! But why?" Anchit asked, looking downright shocked.

"That was the greatest…KISS EVER."

Vimarsh smiled.

"RUN…YOU IDIOT," she yelled.

"BITCH!"

❧◉❧

"So, you asked your doctor friend to prepare a fake medical report on Vimarsh?" Shaila asked.

"Sort of," Nick said.

"You are disgusting."

"If you had known Vimarsh since the time I knew him, you would have been considering me as an angel right now."

"I won't, in any case...Anyway, leave it, but how did he become a hero from a loser?"

"I gave him a burger..."

"So you mean it was a magical burger...bull..."

"No...not the burger...the paper..."

"What paper?"

"The paper in which the burger was wrapped...there was an interview of some guy called Chris who claimed to possess the power to transform anyone within seven days."

"You know that guy? What's his name? Chris?"

"No I don't...but my doctor-friend was a client of his once. Shiva told me that he was good, so I thought I could check it through Vimarsh."

"So you mean to say you knew that Vimarsh would look at the article and rush to meet him? Give me a break...that only happens in movies."

"Well I tried, quite a few times, using various form of tact and situations before nailing the target...and I must tell you it was not easy to do it without arousing suspicion in Vimarsh's mind – slipping the same paper again and again in his hands. I think he was so consumed about his imminent death that our plan worked to perfection."

"So you mean to say that you are the hero?"

"I am only saying that if he is Harry Potter, then I am Dumbledore."

"Anyway...nice work. By the way, what are those marks there and where is HE?"

❦

"Thank God...and you are..."

"Dude, I know."

"No, you are..."

"Yeah...I know it."

"You are really..."

"I know...I am your best friend."

Vimarsh choked with happiness, "But what about the operation and all that pain in my stomach?"

"That is because you failed to drink enough water."

"Water!"

"It was due to stones in your stomach. The doctor was waiting for you to pee...otherwise, the last resort would have been an operation."

"Give me some water."

"Tell Shaila also. Better give her a surprise...ask her to come here," Nick said as he handed over the glass.

"You are right, she must be very worried. I am such a fool. Why did I switch off my cell?" Vimarsh said to himself. He dialled her number.

"Hello Shaila."

"Hi Vimarsh! Where are you *yaar*?"

"I am in the hospital."

"Hospital? What happened? I am coming first now," said she and hung up the phone after checking the address.

"C'mon, hurry up now," Nick said as soon as Vimarsh's call was over.

"Why? Where are we going?"

"Only you are going."

"Where?"

"Ramita is getting married."

"WHAT?"

"Where? To whom? When?"

"This is the address and this is the key of your bike...it is happening right now."

Vimarsh almost jumped up from the bed.

"Wear something...at least," Nick said.

"Who told you about it?"

"She called me two days back, since you were not receiving her calls for the past one week due to all this drama. She asked me to inform you, if I ever met you. She also said that you dare not go to visit her. I think Anchit is the name of the guy she is marrying."

"Nick, I just don't know how much I owe you. You have given me so much...now I want to give you something."

"It is okay, Vimarsh," Nick blushed.

"No, Nick you deserve this."

"What? Why?" Nick exclaimed.

"If she gets married to Anchit...you will have to run for your life...you fuckin'..."

"...Best friend...I know," Nick smiled. "NOW RUN, LOLA! RUN!"

Shaila was laughing as if all hell had broken loose.

"So he slapped you?" Shaila asked amidst laughter. "But why are you at his place?"

"Just wanted to tell someone that I am not that bad as everyone thinks."

"Who?"

"Some girl; you don't know her."

"And why is she important to you?"

"I kind of like her."

"What's her name? Maybe, I could be of some help to you."

"Shaila."

"Yeah, I am listening."

"No...I mean her name is Shaila."

"Oh...same as mine."

"I love you."

"But I don't even know you, forget about loving you."

"Why...even after hearing my story, you don't like me."

"I would still prefer Voldemort; Dumbledore is too old for me."

"What were you doing in the hospital?" Ramita asked.

Vimarsh told her his tale about escaping from near death.

"RASCAL!" Ramita cried out as soon as Vimarsh completed his story.

"Why are YOU saying that?"

"Nick told me that you got married to Shaila to fulfil your mother's last wish, when I called him to ask about you. That's why I asked Anchit to arrange the marriage as soon as possible."

"BASTARD!"

"TOTALLY."

"IDIOT!"

"Who?"

"You."

"Why?"

"How can you believe someone like him?"

"Just as you believed him about your death."

"How did you manage to pull off your wedding preparations at such a short notice?"

"Well, Anchit was scared that I might call off the engagement again, so he decided to go in for the wedding directly. And tomorrow is New Year's Eve, so, in a way, it was perfect."

"Tomorrow is New Year's eve?" Vimarsh remembered the ninety-day challenge and said, "Yes…this is absolutely perfect."

'This I will remember forever…my own mini life,' he thought.

"Now what?" Vimarsh asked after a pause.

"Meet the parents."

"Your parents…where are they?"

"They were at the wedding at which you gatecrashed."

"HOLY CRAP!"

"Ha! Ha! HOLY CRAP," and she hugged him tightly from behind.

Epilogue

"Hello sir."

"I am Chris Mohan. You can call me Chris," he extended his hand.

"Nice to meet you sir...err...Chris."

"Tell me, why are you here?"

"I read about you in a newspaper...I mean about your claim," the man lied.

"So you came here to check my claim?" Chris laughed.

"No, actually I was about to give up my life for a girl when I came across...," the man stopped abruptly. It was better to keep some details only to him.

"So either you mean that the interview saved your life or you think that you can die a few days later after giving me a chance to prove myself."

"No...I mean...I thought I can give it a try," the man said, trying hard to sound convincing.

"You think achieving success is a joke that you can just give it a try and back off at any moment if you don't like the route? Listen carefully mate, I don't do this stuff for money or fame. I have both in enough measure. When I claimed that I can do it, I put my reputation at stake and I won't let any sucker spill the water of failure on it because he wants to give it a try before hanging himself from some bloody ceiling."

"I didn't mean that."

"Then what did you mean? Look mister, I have a seminar to attend and if you can tell me what you really mean by saying it in clear and crisp sentences, it will help a lot both of us in terms of time and energy."

The man felt the same sensation which he usually experienced in front of his love. He kept on looking at Chris with his tongue stuck to his lower jaw.

"Chris, I am fed up with the way I am living. I wanted to achieve a lot in life but when I see it all now, I just hate myself for everything I have done so far. In fact I have done nothing…NOTHING in my life," the man sitting in front of Chris continued. "I could not see any way out of this drain. I love her immensely but don't know how to show to her that I am her true love. If this doesn't change soon, then I will have no other option other than…," he stopped midway in dead silence. He wanted to say much more but he knew that if he continued, he might start crying.

"How?" Chris asked, still looking at him with a calm expression as if nothing had happened in the last five minutes.

"What how?"

"How would you like to kill yourself? By swallowing pills or poison or by some bullets pumped in your head or have you got any other plan?"

"I don't know, I have never thought about that," he lied but was amazed at the response he was getting. He expected either some kind of whacking or preaching in return.

"Okay, we will tell you that. Don't worry about it right now but I want you to answer my question."

He kept on looking at Chris with the same incredulity on his face.

"What do you expect from me? What do you want from me?"

He remained silent for a while as he felt his voice getting choked. The words were hard to find and even harder to utter.

"I want you to show me the way which leads to love and getting loved by one I truly love. I know that there are other ways but there are so many doors to which I don't have the keys. I want your help to unlock them."

"I am still not sure that you can carry the burden of transformation from your present state to the state you want to achieve."

"I will do whatever you ask me to do."

"My fee is too high for individual training."

"I am ready to pay any price," the mortal said, feeling confidence surge inside him. He knew he had nothing to lose now.

"It is not money that I seek but you know what? I will help you. I will teach you the new way of living a happier and prosperous life with the love of your life – a life, where everything is possible and everything will be within your reach. BUT, and this but is a big one. How do I know that you are ready to change and won't step back when the going gets tough? There is something else which you need to do before I accept you under my wings...what is your name by the way?"

"Nikhil. You can call me Nick. I am ready to do any fuckin' thing."

"Never use that word again in this place."

"I am sorry."

"What does your 'anything' include...Nick?"

"I didn't get you."

"Can you KILL SOMEONE?"

Publish with Us:

General Press publishes both, fiction and non-fiction with high standards of production quality. We have a good distribution network of wholesellers and retailers, including online bookstores. Our vision is to provide a platform for Indian writers and bring their work to the market. The intention is to focus all our efforts in bringing quality Indian writing to the Indian market.

We solicit proposals for original and unpublished works for evaluation purposes. Proposals in Hindi and English, in the general and narrative non-fiction categories like self-help, biographies, memoirs, current affairs, business, philosophy, reference, etc., and also fiction in categories such as novels, novellas and short stories are accepted for evaluation by us.

You can mail your proposal to *generalpressindia@gmail.com*.

Your submission to us must contain:

- A detailed synopsis (no more than 2 pages or 700 words);
- The first two chapters and the last one chapter; and
- A one page resume telling us about you, your any published work in the past, relevant writing experience, etc.

* * * * *

If you liked *Emosional Atyachar*, kindly share your reviews on Flipkart.com and Facebook about this book with other readers or send your feedbacks to us.

Illustrated Who Was...? Series (10 Volumes)
by Various Editors

Price : Rs. 1250
Pages : 1120
Size : 7.75x5.25 inches
Binding : Paperback
Language : English
Subject : Biography
ISBN : 9789380914107

Individual Titles are also Available (Rs. 125 each)

Best Gift Item for Children

Illustrated Who Was...? Series is an award winning and international bestselling series, first published in US by Penguin Group. The books have easy do understand text with more than 100 illustrations in each. The series gives a detailed sketch of famous personalities and provides accurate information about them.

Books in this series:

Title Name	ISBN
Who Was Abraham Lincoln?	9789380914008
Who Was Albert Einstein?	9789380914022
Who Was Anne Frank?	9789380914015
Who Was Charles Darwin?	9789380914046
Who Was Leonardo da Vinci?	9789380914091
Who Was Marco Polo?	9789380914084
Who Was Queen Elizabeth?	9789380914060
Who Was Thomas Alva Edison?	9789380914039
Who Was Walt Disney?	9789380914077
Who Was William Shakespeare?	9789380914053

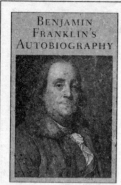

The Autobiography of Benjamin Franklin
by Benjamin Franklin

Price : Rs. 145
Pages : 224
Size : 8.5x5.5 inches
Binding : Paperback
Language : English
Subject : Autobiography
ISBN : 9788190276689

Few men could compare to Benjamin Franklin. Virtually self-taught, he excelled as an athlete, a man of letters, a printer, a scientist, a wit, an inventor, an editor, and a writer, and he was probably the most successful diplomat in American history.

Written initially to guide his son, Franklin's autobiography is a lively, spellbinding account of his unique and eventful life. Stylistically his best work, it has become a classic in world literature, one to inspire and delight readers everywhere. This charming self-portrait has been translated into nearly every language.

Excerpts:

His *Autobiography* thus becomes the first American book to belong permanently to literature. It created a man. The first part written as a moral guide to show his son the way to success, and ensuing parts as a substitute for the treatise on virtue, it offered efficient and firsthand testimony "that man is not even at present a vicious and detestable animal, and still more...that good management may greatly amend him." To think of Franklin as a Romantic, however, is to stretch the limits of that term, for he combined with his confidence in what Emerson later, more enthusiastically, called 'the infinitude of the private man'. Taking what was needed wherever he found it, he was an eighteenth-century man who sifted carefully to discover what was practical and useful and, therefore, best; he made a patchwork of ideas which served him well.

Love Happens only Once...

...rest is just life

by
Rochak Bhatnagar

(Releasing this November)

Brief is Life...
But Love is long...

When his mates were preparing for Board exams, he was busy flirting with girls!!

When his friend wanted to propose a girl, he hasn't even seen, he was busy thinking how to rob his friend's landlord!!

When another friend was searching for a substitute Dad, he was busy kissing his girlfriend in a ladies washroom!!

Meet Rishi and enter into his world full of fun, flirting with random girls, hanging out with friends and his love-interest Ananya.

If you think LOVE is just another four letter word, then think again!!

As after reading this book, your perception about LOVE is going to change from a mere 'Emotion' to 'Devotion'. Because,

Love happens only once...rest is just life...

Price	:	Rs. 100
Pages	:	192
Size	:	7.75x5.25 inches
Binding	:	Paperback
Language	:	English
Subject	:	Fiction/Romance
ISBN	:	9789380914138

A Lot like Love...

...a li'l like chocolate

by

Sumrit Shahi

He's a player. She knows the rules. They meet. Smile. Talk. Add each other on Facebook. Exchange BB pins. He asks her out for coffee. She agrees. Another coffee follows. So do movies, drives, moonlight walks, study dates, sneakouts, make out sessions.

Shadab and Arnika.

Both eighteen. Committed. In a relationship.

It's a perfectly clichéd bubblegum love story...or is it?

For love today comes with a 'conditions apply'.

Career. Ambition. Practicality.

Different colleges. Different countries. Different aspirations.

A long-distance relationship.

They decide to give it a shot. Skype video calling. BBM. Lists of do's and don'ts. Fidelity checks. Promises.

They've planned it all out.

But can love be planned?

Is chocolate a safer proposition for the heart?

Is cheating on your partner an offence only if your partner comes to know about it?

What happens when you're in something which is *A lot like love...a li'l like chocolate*???

Price	:	Rs. 100
Pages	:	192
Size	:	7.75x5.25 inches
Binding	:	Paperback
Language	:	English
Subject	:	Fiction/Romance
ISBN	:	9789380914114